The Gathering Place

"I wonder if his ghostwriting had anything to do with his death," Rachel mused.

"I'm sure the police looked into all the angles."

Ransom Blaisdell had died on March 15. His body was found in his Sherman Oaks living room by his wife, who had just returned from a shopping trip. The police discovered he had been killed by a blow from a "blunt instrument," specifically a bowling trophy on his mantle.

"That's only five days after Uncle Oscar died," Rachel said.

Stu looked at her. "You don't think there's a connection, do you?"

She shrugged. "I don't know. Maybe."

"I'm sure there was nothing funny about your uncle's death. His heart just gave out."

"Oh, I'm sure you're right. I hope you're right. I'd hate to think that Uncle Oscar was . . . but there's no reason to think that.'

JON L.
BREEN
The Gathering Place

WALKER AND COMPANY · NEW YORK

First published in the United States of America in 1984 by the
Walker Publishing Company, Inc.

This paperback edition first published in 1986.

Published simultaneously in Canada by John Wiley & Sons
Canada, Limited, Rexdale, Ontario.

ISBN: 0-8027-3167-8

Library of Congress Catalog Card Number: 83-42914

Printed in the United States of America

10 9 8 7 6 5 4 3 2 1

For Bertha and Harold Gunson,
authors of my favorite work

Prologue. March 10, 1981.

Oscar Vermilion felt tired and old. He knew he wouldn't get any less old, but if he sat for a few minutes in his old leather chair he would certainly get less tired. He tilted his head back and looked at his books, his eyes drifting over their spines. His stock needed dusting. He loved the musty fragrance of this used book store, but not everyone did. Too much dust might lose him customers.

But what did it matter? A customer meant raising his bent body out of the chair, walking to the front to the cash register. How many steps? He'd counted them once. More than thirty-nine.

All seemed past. Alice long gone, so many years ago. Daniel, his son, he could never love except in a father's dutiful way. He'd do right by Daniel in his will, but it was his niece Rachel, lovely girl, who would get what really mattered to him. He thought too much about wills. His life was becoming a documentary, it seemed.

He fingered the pages of the manuscript in front of him. His memoirs. Once an editor had said something of the kind would be publishable. Maybe. But he couldn't do it the way the book world would want it, full of dirt on his famous customers. Not that he didn't know some. No scandal in those pages, except maybe that one thing, and even there he had stopped short of mentioning every name, or that other manuscript that had been left in his care.

Oscar looked at the spines of the books. He could almost see faces on some of them, wavering like dust motes. Fitzgerald, Huxley, Bob Benchley, Nathanael West. All long dead now, and not really replaced. He still welcomed his regulars, but no one could say it was like the old days.

There were nitroglycerine tablets in his desk, the legacy of past heart attacks. But he felt no pain, just tiredness, and the attack came so quickly, he never had a thought of reaching for them.

He would have wanted to spare the customer who found him sitting there dead.

1

March 15, 1981

The writer had seen the obituary for Oscar Vermilion in the paper. And been both saddened and alarmed. Vermilion was a great man, a Southern California tradition, and a trusted friend. Perhaps too well trusted. And now Vermilion's death had brought up an odd question and a problem.

The writer had turned toward the bookshelves in his living room, looking idly at his books in much the same way Oscar Vermilion had looked at his. There was almost as much variety to them, but in this case the writer had written them all himself, every last one.

He looked at the books and wondered how much his guest knew and how to answer the question his guest had posed. "I don't know what to say," he said. "How old Oscar would have known that . . ."

The writer never turned around. The crushing blow on his head was well placed and he died as quickly as Oscar Vermilion.

1. For the last time, and with only slightly mixed emotions, Rachel Hennings walked out of the door of the Tempe bookstore where she had clerked for the last four years while studying for her degree at Arizona State University. She saw Dr. Rodney Wellman's car parked in front of the store. The young psychology professor was waiting to take her to dinner.

And now he was staring at her legs. With dismay.

Rachel had very good legs, but they were seldom on view, and the fact that she'd worn a dress today instead of the usual jeans probably was suggesting to Rodney, quite accurately, that there was something not as usual going on. And Rodney disliked anything that was not as usual.

Rachel steeled herself and fixed a smile on her face. She would have to tell him, and he would take it hard. Their relationship had never been in balance. She regarded him as a friend, and he regarded her as a potential wife. They had first met when Rodney was helping a colleague in the department administer some ESP tests, and Rachel, who had always thought of herself as vaguely psychic, had volunteered to take part. To her disappointment, her score on the test had been somewhat poorer than chance would account for. Maybe, she had joked, that was what it meant to be "vaguely psychic": to have ESP in reverse.

Though Rod was of a conservative bent, it no longer was regarded as unacceptable for a professor to date a student, at least one outside the department. And, as he somewhat pompously pointed out to her, the difference in their ages was only in the single-digit range. To begin with, she was willing to go out with him because she wanted to discuss ESP, the department specialist in the field being middle-aged and married, but Rod had quickly made it clear that his colleague's branch of psychological research struck him as of marginal merit and certainly of little interest to him. Still, somehow the relationship had managed to continue in the three years since that test, Rachel in pursuit of a bachelor's degree and Rodney in more desperate pursuit of tenure. They had seen as much of each other as

Rodney could manage. He had a hard time admitting the relationship was more serious on his side than on hers.

She jumped in the car, leaned over and kissed him lightly on the cheek. "Hi," she said.

"Hi?" he echoed.

"That's a semi-colloquial form of greeting, Professor. I'm sure you must have heard it before."

"Don't go all brittle on me," he muttered and gunned the car away from the curb. He drove three speechless blocks.

"Well?" he said finally.

"You're a scintillating conversationalist this evening, Professor," she said.

"Damn it, Rachel this isn't an ordinary night. What's going on? Why the kissy-face on the way out of the store tonight? Like you never expected to see any of them again? What's going on?"

"For a professor of psychology—"

"Assistant professor."

"—you certainly have unsubtle ways of trying to get information. Couldn't we just go where we're going and sit down over a drink and talk like civilized people? And then maybe if I have something to tell you, I can tell you it, and if you have something to tell me—"

"What would I have to tell you?" he snapped, pulling into the restaurant parking lot.

She looked down at her hands. "Maybe it would be better if we didn't talk at all tonight. But I think we're old enough friends that I shouldn't just leave Tempe without saying good-bye properly."

"You're leaving Tempe?" His voice was not far from a croak. "When? Why?"

"Let me tell you about it inside. I think we both need a drink."

Ordinarily, Rodney would have picked up on that and insisted that he never *needed* a drink. It was a sore point with him because he had had a number of alcoholics in his family.

They entered the foyer of Archie's Steak Factory, starkly tacky-looking on the outside but warm and almost romantic on the inside. A slit-skirted hostess led them to a booth. Her Southwestern friendliness was answered by troubled monosyllables from Rod and a distracted smile from Rachel.

4

Sitting across from Rod and regarding his sad face in the light of the candle on their table, Rachel felt sorry for him and regretted her unsubtle revelation. He had been irritated that things were threatening to go against him, but now irritation had passed and been replaced by desolation. The blow had fallen, and only the details were to be heard.

"You're leaving Tempe," he prompted gently.

"Yes, Rod, I'm afraid so. I'm going to Los Angeles."

"Smoggy and phony."

"Not always and not everybody. And anyway, that won't help. I have to go no matter what. And I want to go."

"What are you going to do there?"

"Operate a bookstore."

He looked up. "You hate the book business. You told me so lots of times."

"No, I never said that. I said I didn't care much for my present job, but that was in a shiny, soulless new book store. I'm going to run a used book store. Vermilion's."

That struck a familiar note. "Vermilion's? You mean . . . but what happened to your uncle?"

She swallowed and looked away. Shaking herself mentally, she took a sip of her drink. "Uncle Oscar died, Rod," she said in a firm, matter-of-fact voice.

"I'm very sorry, Rachel," Rod said. "And I'm ashamed of myself for being so snappy. You know, I get wrought-up at times."

"You should see a psychologist."

"Yeah." He didn't try to smile. "That's very sudden. Had he been ill?"

"He'd had some heart problems in the past, but the last I'd heard he was fine. They said it was a massive heart attack. Probably instantaneous. A customer just found him in the store, slumped over his desk. The way he'd want to go, I guess."

"Are you going for the funeral?"

"I missed the funeral, Rod. He died weeks ago. They just didn't let me know about it until the reading of the will told them I'd been left the store. Here I am one of two living relatives, and I wasn't even notified."

"Who's the other?"

5

"His son, my cousin. A weak-kneed sponge."

Now Rod managed a smile. "That's a terrific mixed metaphor."

"Hey, you *did* take some English courses."

"One or two. So you're going out there to operate the store, huh? You couldn't just sell it?"

"If Uncle Oscar had wanted it sold, he'd have left it to his son and it'd be turned into a video games arcade by now. The store was very special to him. He wanted it continued. He always told me that. And he knew I felt the same way about it. Every time I visited L.A. with my parents when I was growing up, I spent some time in that store with my Uncle Oscar. And that was the highlight. Disneyland and Knott's Berry Farm and Marineland were all very nice, but to me the number-one tourist attraction in Southern California was Vermilion's Bookshop. I loved it. I discovered *The Wind in the Willows* there and the Oz books and even Nancy Drew. Discovered them, Rod, blew the dust off them. Nobody handed them to me in shiny new covers."

Rod shook his head. "I don't get it."

"No, most people don't. I always preferred old books to new ones and old—" she stopped.

"Yeah? What?"

She laughed. "Old people to young ones, I started to say, and that's ridiculous, isn't it?"

"Would you marry me if I were old enough to be my father?" he said quickly, only half kidding.

"This is no time to propose again, Rod. But maybe if you put a little chalk on your sideburns . . ."

"I take it your cousin got the money?"

"He was his son, Rod. Of course he got the money. I'm not concerned about that."

"Don't get me wrong. I don't mean to make you sound mercenary or anything. But we have to look at these things practically. Your Uncle Oscar was a millionaire, right?"

"I suppose so. I guess he must have been."

"So it was perfectly all right for him to jolly himself along running a little used book store, maybe taking a loss on it. But if you're going to run it, make it your livelihood, you have to be sure it's a paying proposition."

6

She sighed. "God, you are practical. I need another drink."

"You don't *need* . . . never mind." He signaled the cocktail waitress and ordered them each another. "Look, Rachel, I am concerned about you. Actually, I think I love you, but I don't mean to lay that on you like any kind of guilt thing. That's my problem. Not that I consider it a problem."

"It's all right, Rod. You don't need to—"

"Yes, I do. Now the fact that I want to marry you and you don't want to marry me, well, that's all right. If I can't be your husband, I can still be your friend. If you're going to go off to L.A. and try to run a business on your own, I want to be sure you aren't heading for disaster. It's something you never have done before."

"The last time I visited Uncle Oscar, when I was seventeen, I spent a lot of time in the store, and he taught me how he did things. It's not exactly a high-pressure business. I can handle it."

"And support yourself?"

"Eventually, I think. I still have quite a bit of the money my parents left me, Rod, and I've scarcely touched it since I've been at State. I could run the shop for at least a year or two just breaking even and do fine."

"But what then?"

"I'll worry about that then. Rod, I know you'd like me to stay in Tempe."

He held a hand up. "Now wait a minute. Of course I'd like you to stay in Tempe. That's obvious. But that's not the point of what we're discussing now. I am a rational adult, and I am accepting your decision, okay? I just want to make sure your decision is on a sound basis."

"Fiscal-wise," she said with a sad smile. "Rod, believe it or not, I was looking forward to a social occasion tonight, not a board meeting."

He snorted. "Yeah, and who elected me to the board anyway?"

"Don't be so silly, Rod. No," she said quickly, forestalling his comment, "I take it back. Mature, rational professors of psychology, even assistant professors, are not silly. It's probably me, and I do appreciate your interest. Now, do we get·anything to eat tonight? You keep waving the waiter away."

7

"Okay, okay. Where is he, anyway? They never come around when you want them."

Both having relatively unemotional stomachs, they managed to enjoy their dinner. An enjoyment of food had kept their relationship going where ESP had failed, and they had shared every kind of eating experience the area had to offer. Tonight's steak-and-seafood place was one of their more conventional choices.

Trying to keep it light, she said, "Remember that chuckwagon place we went to? In the old barn? Where they served the food cafeteria-style on aluminum trays, and they warned you—"

"To grab the tray under the peach? Yeah, I remember." The memory didn't seem to cheer him up any.

"You're really looking forward to this, aren't you?" he said to her over their second glass of wine.

"Yes, I am. It's funny how it never occurred to me that Uncle Oscar would leave me the store. He knew how much I loved it, and all the things he told me about the book business seemed to lead up to this. But it never occurred to me. I never thought of him as dying, either, though he was quite old. Seventy-seven. My parents were only in their late forties when they were killed, but I never thought of Uncle Oscar dying, old as he was. You remember the first time we met? When I volunteered for that ESP test?"

"Of course."

"I was convinced that all sorts of psychic phenomena were whirling around me just waiting to happen. But I'd never predicted anything, never had any presentiment of coming disaster or joy, never thought of a person and then answered the phone and found myself talking to that person, never felt I'd ever been anywhere before."

"Never *déjà-vu*ed anything, huh?"

"Nope. The closest things to real psychic manifestations were things I could never be sure of, and certainly never prove to anyone else. I once woke up in the morning and found I'd finished a term paper in the middle of the night that I had no memory of doing. Automatic typing, I thought, but it was probably just exhaustion playing tricks on me. And sometimes painting a picture I've had the feeling my hand was operating independently of my mind and I'd do something, just a brushstroke or two, beyond my normal talent."

"Automatic painting," Rod said.

"Right. That was probably just mental tricks, too. But I did have this feeling of being psychic somehow. And I thought that ESP test would validate what I'd always thought about myself. But it didn't happen. I was so disappointed. It was in that little bookstore of my Uncle Oscar's that I felt most psychic. Most in tune with the spirits. I'd look at all those books, the newer ones with their bright jackets and the older ones with their beautiful, dignified spines, and I thought of all the famous authors who had visited that store to talk literature and politics and everything else with Uncle Oscar. Most of the ones I thought of were dead—F. Scott Fitzgerald and Nathanael West and Faulkner and Huxley."

"Aldous Huxley? Your uncle knew him?"

"Oh, yes. He died the same day as President Kennedy, did you know that?"

"No."

"Yes, his death went practically unnoticed. Anyway, Rod, you'll think this was funny, but I felt as if they were *there* in the store, watching us, listening to us, taking care of us even."

"The store is haunted?"

"That's how I always felt, though I never really articulated it. Haunted may be the wrong word. It gives some sort of feeling of menace to it, and it wasn't that way at all. The ghosts were strictly friendly ones."

"Like Casper."

"Don't be so cynical, Rod. I felt as if they were there and watching over the store. And I think Uncle Oscar did, too. I think he depends on them to watch over me when I go there, help me make a go of the store."

He looked across the table at her wonderingly. "Do you really believe that?"

She smiled at him. "I don't know. Sitting here with you, I don't suppose I do really, but when I'm in the store again, with those tall shelves looking down on me, I think I might. I hope I will anyway."

He nodded solemnly. "I hope so too." He was beginning to feel the liquor. "You'll keep in touch?"

"I will be a faithful correspondent. I hope you will, too."

"Let me know how things are going, and if you need any help, call my brother Stu at the L.A. *News-Canvas*. He's the book editor there."

"You've mentioned him before."

"Yeah, I suppose I have. Just call on Stu, and you can call on me, too. But I'll be farther away."

"Yes."

The end of the meal was nearing, and she could think of nothing else to say. He apparently couldn't either. He no doubt hoped she would be spending the night with him, but she would have to disappoint him.

At nine o'clock the next morning, Dr. Rodney Wellman was staring into his coffee cup and trying not to jar his aching head. His fingers, remarkably steady, were dialing a Los Angeles number. On the fifth try, he heard a ringing on the other end. The phone service must be improving.

"*News-Canvas,*" said a too-bright voice.

"May I have Stu Wellman's office please?"

"One moment please."

Another assortment of clicks and buzzes.

"Stu Wellman."

"Stu, this is Rodney."

"My long-lost brother. How the hell are things in Australia?"

"Don't be funny."

"You might.as well tell that to Jack Benny or Groucho Marx, Roddy."

"They're dead, and don't call me Roddy."

"So how are you?"

"Hung over. Stu, a friend of mine is coming to L.A."

"Male or female? Must be male, or you'd never tell me about it."

"Female, but she's not your type at all, Stu. She's not blond; she's not brassy; she's not a forty chest. She is kind of beautiful, but it's probably too subtle for you to notice. And anyway, even you have too much class to lay hands on your brother's girl."

"Women aren't property, you know, Roddy."

"That's funny as hell coming from you. Look, Stu, I'm a little worried about her. She's young and she'll be trying to run a business she inherited and she's probably not ready for everything L.A. is going to throw at her."

"She does have her gas mask, doesn't she? And her rape whistle? Also, a hard hat is recommended for this time of year."

"Knock it off. Look, Stu, I just want you to check with her from time to time, make sure she's okay, and give her any kind of help you can. I'd really appreciate it."

"Oh, and I'm sure she'll appreciate the hell out of it, too. Women do like to be checked up on and treated like children these days. All right, I'll do my best. What's her name?"

"Rachel Hennings."

"Do you have an address or phone number where I can reach her? . . . Wait a minute. Did you say Rachel Hennings?"

"Yeah. Do you know the name?"

"I should. It's damned familiar somehow. So where can I reach her?"

"I don't have an address or phone, but the store she'll be running is called Vermilion's Bookshop."

"Eureka! The old geezer's niece. I knew I'd heard the name."

"You knew Oscar Vermilion?"

"Look, brother, I am the book editor of this rag among other overwhelming assignments, and Oscar Vermilion was rather well known in this town in bookish circles. I wrote his obituary. Want to hear it?"

"I listened to enough of your literary efforts when we were kids."

"I have improved."

"But you might just give me the basic facts about Uncle Oscar."

"Uncle Oscar? If you're practically one of the family, you'll know more about him than I do. Let's see. This was from the *News-Canvas* for Wednesday, March 12. The headline reads,

'Vermilion, Local Book Dealer, Dies,' by Stu Wellman, *News-Canvas* Book Editor."

"Goddam it, Stu, this is not a local call!"

"Okay, okay. He was seventy-seven. He'd run the shop on Santa Monica Boulevard for forty-five years. He was found in the shop by a customer on Monday of that week, dead of an apparent heart attack. His shop was a gathering place for writers, mostly those working for the Hollywood film studios. Friends and customers included West, Fitzgerald, Faulkner, Huxley, Bob Benchley, Chandler, Craig Rice, Erle Stanley Gardner, lots more.

"He was born in New York of middle class parents, came to L.A. in 1920. Regarded as a business genius by his contemporaries, he made a bundle in California real estate before he was twenty-five, survived the '29 crash virtually unscathed, and retired to a life of sport and luxury at age thirty. Would I could do the same.

"In 1930, he married the silent movie star Alice Dougherty. Following her sudden death in a 1934 car crash, Vermilion lost interest in most of what his money could buy him—like travel, multiple homes, big cars, yachts, and what he called 'the toys of the overprivileged.' Instead, he decided to devote himself to a 'life of the mind.' Vehicle for said life-style was the small bookshop he opened in 1935. In his later years, he lived in a small Beverly Hills house, modest by millionaire standards. Though a lot of his pile went to charity over the years, it was believed he left an estate valued in the millions.

"Let's see here. During World War II, he intended to sell his shop and join the service, but he was rejected because of his age and slight deafness. One son survived, Daniel D. Vermilion of Santa Monica. His only other relative was a niece, Rachel Hennings, daughter of his late half-sister and only sibling, Roberta Vermilion Hennings. Funeral services were to be private."

"Very private. Rachel didn't even get invited, or told about her uncle's death till after the reading of the will. I wonder why."

"Don't know. Doubt if it's anything too sinister. I interviewed the son, and he doesn't seem the type to be thoughtful about such things. Probably can't see past the end of his own nose.

12

Mind you, that's a fair distance. He could have been called Pinocchio."

"Stu, I have to go to class. God, I'll never make it. You will check with her, won't you?"

"It's part of my beat, Roddy. Hey, she's not a psychology major, is she?"

"No, English."

"Very good. I can't stand psychology majors. Take care, brother."

"Yeah. Thanks. Good-bye."

Rodney Wellman hung up the phone gently. He looked at his watch. She'd be in the air by now. So sudden.

He realized he wanted a drink. But he wouldn't have one. Talking to his brother wore him out, but it also reminded him of all the drunks in the family. Of the whole bunch, only Stu could be funny sober. At least he assumed he was sober.

Poor Rachel. But she'd be okay. Stu and her ghosts would take care of her.

2.

Arlen Kitchener played a mean game of tennis.

His mop of white hair trailed in the wind as he rushed the net. His face red, his expression intense, he smashed the ball to his opponent's backhand with a powerful snap of the wrist. When he saw the ball returned high over his head, deep to backcourt, he almost caught up with it, almost forced still another match point.

Trotting back toward the net, puffing only slightly, he knew that if his opponent had not been a former champion on the professional circuit, she would never have beaten him.

"Nice game, Arlen," said Candy Helms.

"Thank you," he returned, shaking hands over the net. "Your own mastery of this wonderful game is undiminished by the years."

She made a face. "Arlen, please spare me this 'years' stuff."

"My dear, when people can look and play and live younger than they are, it should be a source of pride. Do you know how old I am?"

Candy knew Arlen Kitchener very well. Too well, in fact. Could he imagine she didn't know his age? Nevertheless, she would play the game. "Well, let's see. You play like a twenty-year-old. You have the hard, mature body and strong face that suggests a thirty-year-old. But I'm afraid your prematurely gray hair gives the game away. You simply have to be pushing forty."

"Fifty-five my last birthday," he said proudly. "And you, Candy?"

"Never mind my age."

"Of course. You will, I hope, join me for a drink in the members' lounge?"

"Give me twenty minutes," she said.

Watching his opponent's retreat to the women's locker room, Arlen Kitchener sighed. Her thighs jiggled and she walked like a fashion model. Arlen had reason to know she was good at things other than tennis, but now Candy was simply the perfect opponent for him. The other things were firmly in the past.

Arlen wrapped a towel around his neck and strode contentedly toward the men's locker room. A perfect opponent. Men his own age he could crush, and many younger men he could not stay with. But with her he was perfectly matched. If there was any kind of macho hangup on his part, an ill-suppressed urge to let up against a female opponent or an unreasonable horror at being beaten by one, or if she went all feminine on him and resented his hard shots, then their perfect match would never have worked.

His life was one of perfect matches. He was perfectly matched with his wife, who gave him stability. He loved her, and he knew that his frequent dalliance with other women (which he assumed she knew about, though she never let on) in no way reduced the genuineness or the quality of that love. His first best-seller had been a fictionalized biography of King Edward VII, and he had learned a great deal from that admirable monarch.

He had a perfect match with his agent as well. Clarence Gustavson, a friend from World War II days, had sold his first novel and all the ones thereafter, had even moved west with him in 1956 when the first movie offers came in. Successful authors rarely stayed with the same agent as long as Arlen had stayed with Clarence, but they had never given each other any reason for dissatisfaction. Clarence was a totally honest man, and Arlen placed the highest value on honesty. At least in business matters.

He had a perfect match with his publisher, the same firm these thirty years. He had made them a lot of money, and they had paid him a lot of money, and everyone was happy.

He had a perfect match with his lawyer, Edgar Ferris, whom he saw standing naked under the shower now.

"Good morning, Edgar!" Arlen cried heartily. "Lovely day."

"Hello, Arlen," said the lawyer.

Feeling playful, Arlen considered snapping a towel at Edgar's bare backside. He suspected Edgar would not find it funny, and knowing the eccentricities of your partner was what kept a good match going.

"I almost beat Candy Helms today," Arlen roared, to be heard over the sound of the shower, but still louder than necessary.

"Congratulations," said the lawyer.

"You'll join us for a drink afterwards, I hope?"

Edgar Ferris shook his head, his jowls wobbling. "Have to see a client. Or rather the niece of a former client."

"Ah. Oscar Vermilion's niece, by any chance?"

"Yes, she arrived this morning. I believe she intends to reopen the shop."

"Good news. I always liked that little store. And old Oscar, of course. Is the niece attractive?"

"I haven't seen her since she was eighteen or so. She was attractive then."

"I must drop by the shop in a few days. Give her a chance to get settled first, of course."

The lawyer, frowning, turned off his shower. Though Edgar didn't say anything, Arlen sensed his disapproval of what he would have called Arlen's lecherousness. Under all that dignity and fat, Arlen suspected, Edgar was probably every bit as lecherous himself.

"Give her my best wishes, counsellor," Arlen added, his good humor of the morning easily able to overcome the disapproving aura surrounding the lawyer.

"Yes, I will, of course." Edgar Ferris waddled off.

A few minutes later, Arlen was looking across his margarita at his recent opponent. Candy had been the glamour girl of women's tennis in her younger days, a sort of latter-day Gussie Moran. But Arlen had never found her really attractive then. Only when her adolescent prettiness turned into womanly beauty in her late thirties had Arlen been attracted to her, although he was by no means averse to younger women, even minors. He had been rather foolish over Candy, he knew now, crossed over his usual gentlemanly limits in the pursuit of extramarital affairs. He feared he'd hurt her, though she was a good sport about it. He regretted that tennis could be their only activity now, for Candy (incredibly) was improving with age, seemingly without fighting a desperate holding action against the onrushing years.

"We must do this more often," she said. "You keep my game sharp. And at your age, you're still improving."

Arlen ran a hand through his rich white hair. "I learned it from you, my dear."

"I'm afraid my tennis isn't improving."

"Everything else about you is."

She gave him a full smile. It was dazzling and rare, though her eyes always seemed to be laughing.

"You're very sweet," she said. "A natural athlete with charm. Are you keeping your typewriter warm?"

"Oh yes, finished that article for *Playboy* yesterday."

"*Playboy*," she said mockingly. "I used to have such fun turning them down. And now they don't call anymore." After a pause, she added, "And now I'd say yes."

"They don't know what they're missing. I'll have a word with the photo editor and—"

"Don't you dare!" she laughed. Arlen had practically no sense of humor at all, but she could still have fun with him. "Do you start writing the new best-seller now?"

"Yes," he nodded, quite seriously.

"Arlen, shouldn't you be saying something like, 'I won't know if its a best-seller until it's offered for sale,' or something like that? I wouldn't want you to have any false modesty, but . . ."

"No false modesty about it, my dear. The money my publishers have paid me for it, along with the money a certain film company has already shelled out for it, are the best evidence. It may sound conceited to say that any book with my name on it will automatically become a best-seller, but to be truthful, that seems to be the position. And even if I should write a thoroughly bad book . . ."

He paused so that she could interject, "Which of course is impossible."

". . . my name would still sell enough books to make the best-seller list. What would happen to my next one is another matter."

"And if it didn't sell enough, the flacks from the movie company would go around to all the key bookstores and buy copies like crazy to make sure their prize property got its rightful place on the charts."

"Candy, I see that you understand this business. But I forget you were an actress—"

"Hah!"

"—and an author—"

"Double hah!"

"—in your own right." He stopped a passing waiter. "Two more

17

of the same, Gabe." He continued, "And you must remember, dear, that the term best-seller also refers to a certain kind of book—a certain length, a certain kind of characters, a certain kind of style and plot and situation. It calls for just the kind of thing I have become very good at, that comes naturally to me. I am not a Faulkner or a Wolfe or a Fitzgerald, my dear, but I am certainly a best-seller."

"Can you tell me the plot?"

"Sorry. Never *ever* discuss work in progress. It makes it go stale, you see."

"I see. As an author in my own right, I should know that." She laughed throatily. "And how is Sarah?"

"My wife is flourishing, thank you, simply flourishing."

"And Craig?"

Candy thought she could see Arlen's bright mood dimming suddenly, like a brief power failure. He did his best to keep it going, appealing to back-up generators.

"My son is writing Great Literature. When that blows over, I will teach him how to write a best-seller. I truly think he has the talent for it."

"I'm sure he does. He's an exceptional boy. Tell him I said hello."

"Candy," Arlen said, scowling at his drink, "the boy still has not done an honest day's work in his life. Everything he's got, including the luxury to pretend he's a literary genius, I've given him, and he's perfectly happy to live under my roof and eat my food and drink my liquor, and my dear, I assure you that I don't begrudge him that in the least. But on top of it all, he has no respect for me or for my work. He thinks I have sold out my muse to mammon."

She snickered. "Did he actually say that?"

"No, those were my words, not his. Do they amuse you?" He asked out of curiosity. What amused people interested him.

"Arlen, it's not unusual for someone his age to be like that. He'll change. He'll grow up."

"I know. I keep telling myself that, and Sarah keeps telling me that. But doesn't he see how hypocritical it all is, to live off me and what my writing has made and at the same time to despise it? Of course, he's always talking about moving out, getting a place of his own, making his own way. He *does* think a great writer should have to suffer a bit in order to do really good work, or at least he pays lip service to the idea."

"And what do you say when he suggests that?"

Arlen gulped his drink. "My dear, I do my damnedest to talk him out of it. On the notion that it would somehow be hard on his mother. Sarah, on the other hand, doesn't seem to mind the idea at all. Perhaps I'm as hypocritical as he is. I don't know."

"Arlen, did you know that a newspaper syndicate once approached me about doing an advice column for them? A Dear Abby, Ann Landers sort of thing?"

"Did they?" he said, somewhat absently.

"Yes. I turned them down, of course, but I really think I might be good at something like that, don't you think so?"

He seemed to consider the idea very seriously. "You have a good deal of common sense, and that seems to be all that's required."

"Now, if someone wrote a letter to me about your problem with Craig, I'd tell him that the next time his son says anything about moving out, you—that is, he, his father—should encourage it. The son really wants to stand on his own, but he's too weak to resist when someone opposes the idea."

"You're probably right, dear," said Arlen. "They say children can't choose their parents, but parents can't choose their children either. I've often thought of how perfectly matched I am with the important people in my life: my wife, my agent, my publisher, my tennis opponent. But my son and I are a poor match."

"Give it time. Maybe one of you will improve. Or get worse."

"Another drink?"

She arose. "No, Arlen, I really have to go. Same time next week? For tennis?"

He considered. "For tennis or . . .?"

"Just for tennis, Arlen," she said with a smile.

Because Sarah Kitchener had gone to some kind of charity fashion show that evening, Arlen and his son were alone together for dinner. It seldom happened this way, and they were some-what uncomfortable in each other's company without Sarah there to carry the conversation.

Arlen Kitchener, looking at his son over the dinner table, thought Craig had an unusually weak face. The individual features were all right, but they added up to a lack of character, a lack of forcefulness. The mild blue eyes could rage with self-righteous anger easily enough, but they had no real intensity to them.

Craig Kitchener, looking at his father, saw a cold and humorless tyrant, with a face unreachable by reason and emotion.

To an objective observer, they looked enough alike facially to be identical twins, or anyway older and younger brother.

On these occasions, it seemed they could only communicate by arguing, only break the ice with a sledgehammer. Each would have denied he wanted it that way, but the denials would ring hollow. It wasn't far into the meal that their voices began rising.

"Get any work done today, son?" Arlen began it mildly enough.

"Yes, I work every day. I have to. I'm driven to."

"Driven to! I think that machine still has the original ribbon."

"*I'm* not a goddam machine, dad. It comes slow for me. And the surroundings here are all wrong for writing of substance. For writing crap, they're apparently terrific."

"You're an offensive little creep," said Arlen, whose son out-weighed him by forty pounds.

"Okay," said Craig, tilting his head back and regarding his father down his nose, a mannerism Arlen found almost as offensive as his son's conversation. "Let's talk nice. What did *you* do today? Did you get the old Selectric humming?"

"Son, when you get to a certain point of self-discipline and successful craftsmanship, it is possible to take an occasional day off. I had a game of tennis."

"With Candy Helms?"

"Yes."

"You still fucking her?"

"Craig, I will thank you not to use such language in this house."

"Why not? Mother isn't here."

20

"Even so. This is her house, and that kind of talk defiles it."

"What about that kind of action?"

"You are too young to understand the complexities of life and relationships, son, however smart you may think you are. And whatever I have done in my life, I have never done anything under this roof that I could be ashamed of."

"I could name about six novels you wrote under this roof—"

"Oh, just shut up! I don't know why I take all this from you, I really don't. Why do you stick around here?"

Craig smirked. "For mother's sake. We've established that."

"I think the time has come that you should be out on your own, and I don't think your mother would stop you with any great insistence. If you think you could become a great writer starving in a garret, then go and starve in a garret for a while. Maybe you're right. Maybe if you didn't have to write under my roof, you wouldn't write such crap. Maybe if you stay here too long, you'll end up writing like me. You'd make a bit of money, but you'd tear your principles to shreds, wouldn't you, son?"

Craig sat back in his chair and put down his napkin beside his plate. These sessions were hell on the digestion, and somebody had to back off from the shouting.

He said in a lower voice, "You know, dad, the thing of it is you could write something good now. With all the money you have and all the additional money just your name can command, you could take advantage of it and really do something worthwhile. But do you? No, you just write the same old stuff."

"I can remember when you liked what I wrote."

"Can you?"

"Can't you? I remember the first book of mine you read you thought was terrific."

Craig nodded his head slowly. "That's right. I remember, too. I read it when I was fifteen. I wasn't even allowed to read your books before that. Mother wouldn't let me read that kind of stuff. Isn't that a laugh? But yes, I remember that one book. Do you remember which one it was?"

Arlen thought for a moment. "No, I can't", he said with a slight smile.

"I'm surprised you can't. It was the only good book you ever wrote, dad. That one book was something to be proud of. In a lot of ways, it was no different from the others, but it had some real substance to it. Can't you remember? Surely you remember what your own best book was?"

"Opinions may differ on that point, you know. But go ahead and enlighten me. Which book was it?"

"Your own fifteen-year-old loved your book and you don't even remember which one it was?"

The decibel level was rising again.

"Look, kid, stop trying to pile guilt on me. I've been a good father to you. I've given you everything."

Craig snickered weakly. "Not quite everything. But forget it. I don't want to argue anymore. I get sick of it."

"Well, which book was it? At least tell me that."

"*The Atlantis Courier*. Corny title, but a hell of a book. I read all your other books after that, and I was disappointed that none of them were up to that first one. I read the thing again last summer, dad. It was a good book. It made a good statement about pollution and prejudice and all kinds of other contemporary evils. In your other books, there's nothing like that."

Arlen was silent for a moment. He took another mouthful of now cold roast beef, not because he wanted it but to demonstrate that this conversation wasn't having any great effect on him. Then he said thoughtfully, as if it really didn't matter, "I didn't think *The Atlantis Courier* was such a good book. It was all right, but not anything special."

"That I liked it doesn't make it special?"

"Sure, son, I value your opinion. You know that."

"I *know* that? Pardon me while I laugh in your face."

Craig rose and stormed out. Arlen stared sadly at the remains of his dinner. Tomorrow night the boy's mother would be back at the table and the gloves would be back on, thank God. Arlen couldn't take much more of this goddam encounter therapy.

Why did it have to be *The Atlantis Courier* Craig had liked? Why couldn't it have been any other book but that?

3. Rachel was tired. It didn't seem too logical, really. How much of a case of jet jag could a person get flying from Phoenix to Los Angeles? But it had been a biggish day.

Her cousin Daniel, in a surprising if grudging gesture, had met her at the airport. He had even gracelessly offered her a room to stay in at his home until she could find a place of her own.

"It's what the old man would want me to do, Rachel," Daniel said, in the tone of a man faced with an unpleasant but necessary duty. "He thought a lot of you, you know. You and he were like a couple of bookends. I live in the real world, though, so he and I never seemed to get along too well. Hard to understand how he made all that money, but that was before we knew him, huh?"

Finding her cousin's company no more congenial than she had when she had first taken a dislike to him—at age six, if she recalled correctly—she had declined. In the afternoon, she had rented a car, seemingly the only feasible means of transportation in Southern California, and driven to lawyer Edgar Ferris's office to discuss some matters connected with the estate. The amount of paperwork involved shouldn't have surprised her, but it seemed beyond her most pessimistic expectation.

The formalities concluded, Ferris sat back at his desk and looked at her. She seemed very young to him, very fragile. Though she was obviously intelligent, she surely could not have much experience of the business world.

"You know," he said tentatively, "the bookshop was the most important thing in Oscar's life. But it was hardly a paying proposition for him. I believe he broke even at best, and of course he did not have to do any better. He did not depend on it for his livelihood, having taken care of that half a century ago."

"Yes, I understand," she said, expecting a repeat of Rodney Wellman's financial lecture.

"I imagine you could sell the stock of the store for a quite nice price. And the building, which of course Oscar owned outright and has now bequeathed to you, is a valuable item as well, as is the land it stands on. I don't know your own financial position,

Rachel, and I admit it's none of my business. But I should think that selling the store would be a much more, uh, prudent action than continuing to operate it as a bookshop. That's merely my opinion, of course."

"I appreciate it. But I don't think Uncle Oscar left me the store with the idea that I would sell it."

"No, no, certainly not. I agree. But I can't help feeling he would understand if you came to a decision . . ."

"I'm not sure that he would," she said with a serene smile. "I am going to reopen the store, Mr. Ferris, and operate it as best I can for as long as I can. If it doesn't work out, well, at least I will have tried."

Edgar Ferris nervously cleared his throat. "Of course. Well, if I can be of any help to you, I'll be more than glad . . . well, I'm sure you know that. And your uncle had a good many friends in the local literary community, who would no doubt be pleased to help out as well."

"Thank you."

Ferris shrugged his massive shoulders. "As to the location, I think it is reasonably good. Santa Monica is a well-traveled street. But you may be surprised to find that yours is the only, ah, legitimate book dealership on that particular stretch. Many of the neighboring businesses are so-called adult bookstores, massage parlors, things like that. The shop is as pleasant as ever, but the surroundings are not what they once were."

"I understand," Rachel replied. "I don't think Vermilion's is movable, though. The store *is* that building, that location. I can't imagine moving it to Hollywood Boulevard, somehow."

Edgar Ferris smiled. "That street is not what it once was, either. But then, what is?"

"Yes." Since Ferris seemed so sympathetic, she almost said something about the move displacing the ghosts that lived in Vermilion's, but she decided it was better if the laywer didn't have any reason to doubt her sanity.

"And will you be staying with Daniel Vermilion?"

"Uh, no, it was kind of him to offer, but I'd rather be on my own. Is that apartment over the shop occupied at the moment?"

"Why, no. Your uncle hadn't rented it out for several years

before his death. He preferred to have it as a second base of operations. Sometimes he chose to spend the night there rather than to return home. Are you planning to stay there?"

"I think I'd like to, yes. It would be very convenient."

"It could be dangerous, too, living alone there. Still, it would be a financially sound move."

She laughed. "Well, if it's a financially sound move, then to hell with the danger."

Edgar Ferris didn't laugh. "You should know that there has been at least one break-in there since the store has been closed."

Rachel was concerned. "Was there a lot of damage?"

"No, but someone made quite a search of the place. I can't imagine what they were looking for. Of course, if there were any books missing, I'd never know. I've had the locks changed and the place is quite secure now. I also had the books replaced on the shelves as well as possible, and when you go there you'll hardly know there had been a burglary. Still, it should make you think twice about actually living there. It was a curious sort of burglary, really. A closed bookstore seems an odd place to burglarize."

"Well, it must have been a booklover who was impatient waiting for Vermilion's to reopen. I don't feel threatened by that, Mr. Ferris. I mean, it's part of big-city life, isn't it?"

"Well, I suppose most businesses encounter crime sooner or later. Still, I hope you know what you're doing," the lawyer said. "Apart from the question of living there, there is the larger question of your reopening the store. I wonder if you've considered all the fiscal implications."

"Do you know Rodney Wellman by any chance?"

"Who? No, I—"

"Mr. Ferris, I'm not sure I want to consider quite all the fiscal implications. I don't want anything or anybody to talk me out of operating Vermilion's."

"You might consider some moves to put the shop on a securer footing, like serving food, for example."

"Serving food in a bookshop?"

"Some small shops along the coast do it now. Perhaps, shifting to a new stock, not those dusty old secondhand books Oscar dealt in. And you could serve tea or coffee, and light snacks, not full meals, of course. A sidewalk cafe ambiance. Poets and things."

She looked at him blankly.

"It's quite the coming thing. And I can't help thinking you need something."

"Like a gimmick? No, Mr. Ferris, I want to run Vermilion's and keep it as it always was. Pour a cup of coffee or a drink for a special guest, fine. That was my uncle's tradition. But to make it into a commercial fast-food operation . . ."

"I wasn't suggesting quarter-pounders or fish and chips, and a bookshop *is* a commercial operation. But never mind, it was just a suggestion."

There were several more minutes of well-meant warnings and suggestions before Rachel acquired the most important objective of her meeting with Edgar Ferris: the key to Vermilion's. Ferris offered to accompany her there, but she was determined to rediscover the shop on her own. With a feeling of edgy anticipation, she drove her rental car to her new home and business.

The neighborhood didn't seem so different. Yes, there were some disreputable-looking "adult" bookstores (with a stock far more juvenile—or infantile?—than Uncle Oscar's) and massage parlors. But there were also discotheques and restaurants and specialty shops. And Santa Monica Boulevard was wide enough to give a feeling of open space; it did not offer the claustrophobic feel of sin centers in cities like New York and London. In broad daylight, it did nothing to make Rachel feel uncomfortable.

And the shop looked no different. Housed in its own two-story building, narrow but relatively deep, with a sloping roof suggestive of a snowier climate and weathered red wood that made her think of an unusually attractive old barn, Vermilion's Bookshop had retained the warmth and charm it had always held for her. Rachel felt a tightness in her throat and a moisture in her eyes at first sight of it, but she mentally gave herself a shake. Sentimental nonsense would be unproductive at this point.

She found a place to park directly in front of the shop. That could only be a good omen.

Uncle Oscar had frequently changed the exhibits in his small display window. At the moment, along with a rather forlorn

CLOSED sign, the window displayed some children's books: several of the Oz series, an early Hardy Boys, a couple of Tom Swifts. A pleasant display, but obviously very dusty.

Rachel unlocked the door with one of the keys Ferris had provided. The door swung open rather hard, as if warped by the spring rain. The bell on the door jingled, and it was almost impossible to believe Oscar Vermilion would not come bustling out to greet his visitor.

There was a small desk just inside the front door. It had a locked drawer in which change, checkbooks, receipt books, mailing labels, and other items necessary to the running of a bookstore were kept. There was also a selection of bookmarks, imprinted with the name and hours of Oscar Vermilion's store. Just opposite the desk, on one of the shelves that extended the length of the shop, was a small bulletin board affixed with newspaper articles and flyers proclaiming various literary events taking place the week of Uncle Oscar's sudden death.

Rachel remembered that the light switches were at the back of the shop. Locking the front door behind her, she inched slowly toward the back, leaving the light seeping through the front window and moving farther and farther into darkness. Once she had been trapped after-hours in a far corner of a university library, and the experience had been terrifying. The darkness of Uncle Oscar's shop held no threat for her, however. She felt at home here, among beniferent spirits if any.

Finally she found the lights, near the back wall. This was the part of Uncle Oscar's shop she remembered with the most fondness: the middle shelves did not reach all the way to the back of the store, and there was a grouping of easy chairs around a circular coffee table. The chairs, old and inviting black leather, had been the gathering place for Uncle Oscar and his literary cronies. Nearby was a locked cabinet, repository of Vermilion's liquor supply. In one corner was a rolltop desk with a shelf of reference books. Included was the current edition of *Books in Print*. Though Vermilion's did not stock very many new books, Uncle Oscar would often special-order for his customers. This was where Oscar Vermilion had done most of the real business of the shop, carrying on correspondence and pricing books.

As Edgar Ferris had promised, she saw few signs of the burglar's activities. Looking closely, though, she could see the lock on the liquor cabinet had been replaced. It still seemed well stocked with bottles, though.

Rachel missed one thing. Uncle Oscar had always kept plants in the store, usually ones that could live happily without much sun. Apparently someone, presumably not the burglar, and more likely lawyer Ferris than her cousin, had been kind enough to rescue them and save her the unpleasantness of greeting a forest of dead houseplants when she entered the store. Now she could either arrange to get the original ones back or procure some new ones.

Rachel took the back stairs up to the second-floor apartment. There was also an outside entrance, used when Uncle Oscar had rented it out, but she would use the inside stairway from the store. The apartment was rather sparsely furnished, but it had the necessities, and she soon satisfied herself that everything worked, including the small refrigerator and a vacuum cleaner. Had the burglar been up here, too? Edgar Ferris hadn't said. Still, why would lightning (or burglars) strike twice in the same place?

Shaking off thoughts of unwelcome visitors, Rachel occupied herself with making a list of provisions she would need to procure from a local supermarket. She also opened every window she could and let the freshest air Santa Monica Boulevard could provide circulate through the small apartment.

There was a lot to think about and a lot to do to get the shop rolling again. She realized she was rather insistently facing the entire matter alone. But she was that type of person. Solitude had never really bothered her. And anyway, how could she feel really alone in Vermilion's Bookshop?

When the telephone rang about five o'clock of that first afternoon, the sound was not welcome or friendly. It seemed like an intrusion. Probably it would be Edgar Ferris' office and more paperwork to worry about.

"Hello."

"Uh, hello. Is this Rachel Hennings?" A pleasant and youngish male voice.

"Yes, it is."

"You're going to think this is rather strange, I know, Ms. Hennings, but I have this brother, you see . . ."

She brightened. "Are you Stu?"

"Wow! You must be one of these psychics."

"Not necessarily. You're the only person in Southern California I know who has a brother. Or whose brother I know. Or something like that."

"Yeah. Well, anyway, I want to welcome you to our city. I know you will like it here and make a big success of reopening Vermilion's. My brother has this quaint idea that you might need someone to act as a guardian angel or something, and while I'm sure you can more than take care of yourself, I just wanted you to know that I'm available to help you any time you need my help."

"That's very nice of you, Stu. Why don't you call me Rachel?"

"Gee, I don't know," said the voice with gloriously phony earnestness. "You are my brother's girl, after all."

"But this is Southern California. And you've already made the political point with that 'miz.' "

"Yeah, I guess you're right. Well, look, when are you planning to open up the store again? I can probably put something in the paper about it. Vermilion's is something of a local landmark, you know, in some circles. It's true that ninety-nine percent of the people who read the *News-Canvas* have never heard of it, but then they never read the book page anyway."

"I'm not sure. But I'll let you know."

"Well, you know, anything I can do to help."

"Thanks very much, Stu, I appreciate it. And by the way, I'm nobody's girl."

"Of course not. A poor choice of words. You're my brother's woman. No, that's not right either. You're your own woman."

"Yes, I like that. Stop right there."

A moment later, she hung up the phone laughing. He certainly didn't sound much like his brother Rodney. She wondered if he was always so unrelievedly facetious and jocular.

For several hours she occupied herself with cleaning up the apartment, buying a few groceries, eating a light dinner, though she wasn't really hungry. Now it was getting toward eight o'clock, and she was feeling the effects of the day. The traffic noise seemed very loud to her, and she knew it was something she would have to get used to it if she expected to sleep nights here. Her apartment in Tempe had been quiet, and what noise there was had come from neighbors holding parties, not a problem here.

Tired, yes, but not sleepy. She was still too keyed up, and she knew how much work was ahead of her. She didn't feel she could work any more tonight, but she could creep down to the shop and find something to read.

Descending the stairs, she discovered that the fifth one from the top creaked loudly. It would tell her when the burglar was coming back. But, don't be silly, the burglar wasn't coming back. She made a mental note to skip that step whenever possible. Halfway down, it occured to her that a downstairs light on the landing would be nice in order to avoid going downstairs in darkness. Reaching the bottom, she switched on the light nearest to her and the back of the shop lit up, illuminating the last few sections of shelving on the wall, the rolltop desk, and the circle of black leather chairs. It was much quieter down here, as though the shelves of books intercepted the traffic noises from the street outside.

She noticed one stack of books alongside the rolltop desk. She picked up the top one, opened it to the front endpaper, and noticed that there was no price there in Uncle Oscar's small and neat hand. Obviously, these were new acquisitions he hadn't got around to pricing before his death. The book on top was a first edition of James Gould Cozzens' *The Just and the Unjust*. She smiled. Uncle Oscar had always joked about that book, claiming it was the most common American first edition by a major author and that he sometimes stumbled across half a dozen copies a day.

The second book looked promising. Ernest Hemingway's *A Farewell to Arms*. She quickly turned to the verso of the title page. Second printing! She plucked one of the reference books off the shelf on the rolltop desk. It was a few-year-old edition of Van Allen Bradley's *The Book Collector's Handbook of Values*. She looked under Hemingway and saw that a first of *A Farewell to Arms* would have been worth $75 or more. Impulsively, she also turned to the entry for James Gould Cozzens. Unsurprisingly, *The Just and the Unjust* wasn't in there, but the book informed her that for Cozzens' first book, *Compulsion*, she could charge $125 or more. That was if she had one, of course.

She looked at the other books in the stack. There was a copy of F. Scott Fitzgerald's *The Great Gatsby*, published in 1925. No dust jacket but in nice condition. Consulting Bradley, she saw that the first could bring $100, five times that if it had its jacket, and that she could check whether it was the first issue by checking for a misprint on line nine of page 205. With trembling fingers, she did so, and sure enough, the phrase "sick in tired" appeared there. It was the first.

But how much would she sell it for? Uncle Oscar had never charged premium prices for his books, and she didn't want to alienate his old customers by becoming a clip joint. She carried the book and several others in the stack over and sat in one of the black leather chairs. She placed the books on the round card table in front of her.

She felt drained. This was no time to think about matters of commerce. She was too weary. Pricing policy she could think about tomorrow.

She picked up the copy of *The Great Gatsby* with its dark green cloth, weighed it in her hand. It had been one of Uncle Oscar's favorite novels. She had read it, too, in a tattered paperback edition. That burglar mustn't have been much of a book person, or he would have taken this with him. Unless he had already stolen a Gutenberg Bible and a first folio Shakespeare, and *The Great Gatsby* would have made the load too heavy. Forget that damn burglar, she told herself. He's forgotten you.

And then it struck her that F. Scott Fitzgerald had often been a customer in her uncle's shop. In his later days, of course, long after he was the literary idol of the twenties, the chronicler of flaming youth. When he'd visited Vermilion's, he was a middle-aged alcoholic, sometimes on and sometimes off the wagon, struggling quite sincerely to be a successful screenwriter. He was an unhappy man, his books out of print, but he had been a wonderful conversationalist, and discussing life and literature with Uncle Oscar and the other authors that frequented the shop had often lifted his spirits.

Quite likely, he had sat in this very chair at one time or

another. Long before Rachel's time, of course. . . . What would it have been like to have sat here and discussed everything under the sun with Fitzgerald and Nathanael West and the rest?

Taking a deep breath, Rachel let her eyes roam over the high shelves of books that lined the wall. How many books were there? And how many authors? How many of them were alive and how many dead? How many died in bed in old age, and how many killed themselves like Hemingway or died in auto crashes like West? How many of them had sat in these chairs around this table? She almost felt they were there with her. She almost felt she could hear them talking. The lower shelves threw odd shadows on the walls, like ghosts hovering in the air, but they held no terror for her. They were friendly.

Rachel stood up and walked to her uncle's rolltop desk. She wondered if there was a fountain pen. She opened a drawer, saw several ballpoints and one lone fountain pen, with a little jar of ink. She tested the pen on a piece of scratch paper and saw that it had ink in it. That was a good thing, for she had never used a fountain pen in her life and had no idea of how to fill one.

She walked back to the table and sat down again.

What did I want this for? she wondered. Uncle Oscar always marked his prices in pencil.

Her right had reached out and opened the cover of *The Great Gatsby*. She watched it with interest, strictly a spectator, feeling somewhat as she had those times when her hand seemed to paint a few brushstrokes independent of her will. Now that same mysteriously guided hand took up the fountain pen and began to write something in the book.

She was briefly horrified. What am I doing? I'm defacing a valuable first edition. I must be crazy. Then she saw what she had written.

In a hand completely unfamiliar to her was a signature:

F. SCOTT FITZGERALD

Her eyes wide, she thought the proper response would be to recoil in horror or scream or faint. But she did none of these things.

This was Rachel Hennings' first demonstration of her unusual talent.

4. A week passed before Rachel felt ready to reopen Vermilion's. In that time, she led an odd, solitary existence. She turned in the rental car and managed without one, unheard of in Southern California. She filled the shop with plants again, dusted the shelves and most of the books. When she found one less dusty than the others, she found herself speculating that the nocturnal visitor must have removed it from the shelf.

Her unexpected and unexplained ability to sign the names of dead authors to copies of their books bothered her. It was not, she soon found out, confined to duplicating the signature of F. Scott Fitzgerald. She could autograph the books of many different authors, in many very different hands.

Periodically, the strange talent demonstrated itself as she sat thumbing through the old books at Uncle Oscar's desk. A part of her was delighted and a part of her was worried, but all of her was baffled by it. Yes, she believed in ESP and other paranormal phenomena, indeed had a strong interest in them. And she felt that whatever spirits might inhabit this shop were beneficent ones. But any loss of control of one's actions is troublesome, and something in her did not like the sensation of her hand doing something that was not directed or even understood by her head.

The talent led her to reread (or sometimes read for the first time) the works of that group of writers she had gathered at Vermilion's, and it was like reading the books of friends. She knew the signature phenomenon was a form of automatic writing, but it was a type she had never heard of before. She searched the shelves for books on the subject, but the occult had never been one of Uncle Oscar's specialties, and soon she went beyond the Vermilion's stock to continue her research in the public library. She read of many astonishing and (at least according to the authors) well-documented cases, but none just like her own.

She managed to shop for food and needed business supplies and continue her research with a minimal use of the scarcely adequate Los Angeles public transportation system. Usually she walked, also unusual in Southern California. If she had put on a sweatsuit and jogged, no one would have thought it odd, but walking brought some puzzled and amused stares her way.

She got to know a few of her fellow merchants along that particular stretch of Santa Monica Boulevard, and whatever their trade, they seemed friendly and helpful.

At the end of the week, Vermilion's looked as pleasant as ever, ready to welcome Uncle Oscar's old customers and (she hoped) many new ones. Quietly, without a call to Stu Wellman or any other kind of public announcement, she reopened the shop. Gradually, book lovers rediscovered Vermilion's, and a varied and usually delightful lot of them began to put in appearances in the store.

As she introduced herself to the used book business, Rachel discovered more and more differences with the comparatively sterile new book business. There seemed to be as many collecting interests as there were customers. Uncle Oscar had some old paperback reprints, mostly mysteries, with maps on the back covers; he had put them in individual plastic bags and priced them at two dollars each. A surprising number of customers seemed to find them a bargain at this price. Other paperback collectors turned up their noses at the map-backs but looked for the works of certain illustrators, or wanted only books (regardless of content) whose covers depicted bondage, bestiality, or some other sexual symbolism, subtle or overt.

There were, of course, traditional first-edition collectors, working on certain specific authors or periods. But there was also a grave young man who quite seriously collected second editions, pronouncing them much rarer than firsts. One elderly lady actually collected *Reader's Digest Condensed Books*. With all that were available at thrift shops and library book sales, it was a wonder she ever felt the need to enter Vermilion's.

Most of the customers were not collectors at all, just people looking for something good to read at a reasonable price. And these were her favorites, as she thought they had been Uncle Oscar's. She couldn't imagine owning a book without intending to read it, whatever further value it might have as a collector's item. The difference between books and other collectibles was content. If you had no concern for content, you might as well be collecting stamps or coins or beer cans.

Some collectors seemed compulsive and eclectic. There was the man who walked into the store with sidstepping reluctance, as if he were being sucked in by some force stronger than himself. "I'll just look around," he said. "I can't possibly buy any more books. I have a garage full of them, boxes stacked to the ceiling. I've figured out that I'm forty now, and if I read one book I own a week, I still won't be finished by the time I'm ninety. A book a week may not sound like much, but I'm a slow reader. But I just like to look around anyway." He left the shop with an armload of bargains and was back the next day.

Not all her customers were as pleasant, of course.

There were the customers who demanded a paperback edition of a best-seller that had come out a week before in hardback only. This type wasn't discouraged even when she told them hers was a used book store only. Then they would ask if she had a used copy of the paperback of the hardback best-seller.

Sometimes book buyers would expect the store to be nothing short of a major research library in the magnitude of its holdings. They would stare in shocked disbelief when told Rachel didn't have a copy in stock of the 1928 UCLA yearbook or a 1952 *World Almanac* or a complete run of the U.S. Department of Agriculture publications or a single obscure Tom Swift or Bobbsey Twins book. And she called this a bookstore?

More troubling was a forty-ish man with a beard who appeared at the shop two or three times in the first week. He said little, always bought something with the air of not caring what, and seemed to be looking around for something else. Why did he keep coming back? His intensity led Rachel to identify him in her mind with the mysterious burglar, though she knew there was no sound reason to do that. He didn't have an air of menace exactly, but he seemed to be a man with a purpose who had lost a sense of how to gain that purpose.

Sometimes Rachel had the feeling that the bearded man was about to take her into his confidence, explain what it was that was bothering him. But, apart from one unfruitful exchange about some travel books, their conversation never passed beyond the may-I-help-you-I'm-just-looking stage.

Fortunately, relatively few customers were so troubling, and running the bookshop was as much fun as she had hoped.

But one thing continued to bother Rachel: what to do about those signed books. Worst of all, she sometimes even found herself wondering whether they were real or an illusion. Could they all be products of her imagination? Could anyone else even see these ghost signatures? She hadn't tried to show them to anyone and certainly hadn't offered any for sale.

Finally it occurred to her where she might go for help.

When Stu Wellman had been given the job of book review editor on the Los Angeles *News-Canvas,* the city's number-three daily and sinking fast, he had imagined it as an opportunity to do a lot of reading on the job. It hadn't turned out that way. For one thing, the book editorship was anything but a full-time job. He was still expected to handle other general reporting assignments. Though he would have liked to have a weekly book review section to fill, like the one the rival *Times* put out every Sunday, he had to be content with a page on Sunday and two short midweek reviews. Most of these he was expected to farm out to other reviewers, preferably big names, so he rarely had the chance to write a review himself. And pressure from his colleagues for free review copies of the latest books was great.

The weekly "Book Chat" column he was charged to produce involved much perusal of publisher's publicity copy and phone calls to agents and publishers and writers and book dealers to get the latest scam, but it involved little more reading than writing a Hollywood gossip column would have.

As usual this particular morning, his desk in the city room was piled high with shiny new books and occasional sets of galleys. He first tried to separate them into the reviewable and the disposable. The first group he put aside for closer consideration, the challenging task of picking the right reviewer. The second group went on a side table near his desk where any employee who was attracted to them could take them home. A third, between-two-stools sort of group were put in a small pile under Stu's desk and would be taken home to become a part of his own regrettably little-read library. Stu could keep what he wanted, give away what he wanted, but selling the copies to a dealer for his own profit had been explicitly designated out of bounds by his editor.

In the midst of this sorting, the com-line on Stu's desk phone buzzed, and he picked up the receiver.

"Wellman," he said.

"Call for you on line one, Stu," said the switchboard operator's sexy voice. She was a fifty-year-old grandmother who sounded like a starlet.

"Friend or flack?"

"Not a flack, I don't think. You'll have to decide if she's a friend."

He punched line one on his phone and repeated, "Wellman."

"Hello, Stu. This is Rachel Hennings."

"Rachel? Hennings? Do I know you? Oh, yes, what's new in the old book business?"

"Well, I'm open. Vermilion's has been back in business for a week."

"A week? That's fine, but you should have let me know ahead of time. I'd have given you a plug in the column."

"I hope you still can."

"Oh, I'll try. But you have no idea how tough it is to find space for an item about *used* books. It doesn't impress the guys trying to sell new books, or our advertising department, one bit. But for you, a friend of my brother Rodney, I'll do it."

"What do you hear from Rod?"

"I never hear from Rod. He writes a letter about as often as William Styron writes a novel."

"I hope you'll come by the store sometime and have a look. I'd like to meet you. Call it the official grand opening."

"You're serving champagne, of course."

"No, but you're welcome to bring some. Actually, Stu, there is something I'd like your advice on. I have some books that appear to be signed by their authors, and I think they might be forgeries. Do you know of anyone who could authenticate them for me?"

37

"I know an autograph dealer, yes. Why do you think they're forgeries?

"Uh, I'd rather not say just now. But I would like someone's opinion of them. And I'd rather not go to anyone about it directly myself. I know it's a lot to ask, but I thought you'd know someone."

"Of course. No trouble at all. And if we're talking about book forgery—"

"Not book forgery. Just autograph forgery."

"Even so, there might be a story in this for the paper, mightn't there?"

"No!" she said quickly. "There won't. You have to promise me not to write about this, whatever happens."

It surprised Stu that anyone would call a reporter on something like this and expect to avoid publicity. But, on the other hand, what chance was there that there would be any publicity value to it? She was probably just an overly cautious book dealer. So he agreed.

Stu had last visited Vermilion's shortly after the death of old Oscar. Today it seemed subtly different, brighter, tidier, more welcoming, the aura of death vanquished. He swung open the door, hearing the bell jingle over his head. There were no customers in evidence and for a while no proprietress. Antiquated word, he considered.

When she did appear, she surprised him. Rod's almost apologetic description of her led him to expect a rather mousy sort of girl, but she was anything but. Her shoulder-length brown hair was lustrous, her somewhat heart-shaped face lovely, her green-gray eyes intense and startling. What she did for the faded blouse and blue jeans she wore suggested a woman who would look elegant in rags.

She looked tired, though, with dark circles under the lovely eyes. Something was troubling her.

"Are you Stu?" she asked somewhat warily.

"Yeah, Rachel. Good to meet you at last. How are you?"

"Fine," she said. "You don't look like I pictured you."

"Like you pictured me. Let's see. Identical to Rodney, but with a cynical smirk on my face, a pencil on my ear, bags of dissipation under my eyes, and no thick-lensed glasses. Right?"

"Right," she said. "And reporters are supposed to wear hats, too."

Truthfully he didn't look enough like Rodney to be his brother. Maybe one of them was adopted. Stu was tall, thin, and blond, where Rodney was short, bulky, and dark. Finally, she decided the largish, somewhat pointed nose, far less at home on Stu's almost gaunt face, was the key clue to their fraternity.

"This doesn't look much like a grand opening," Stu remarked.

She smiled. "I want to ease into this business gradually. I don't want to be a media event. In fact, on thinking it over, I'm not sure I even want a mention in your column."

He gave her a crooked grin. "I hate to tell you this, but the effect would be somewhat less than a notice the Rolling Stones were staying at Motel 6. I don't think you'd be overrun with curiosity seekers. Maybe if I ran your picture with the item, but even then . . ."

She laughed. "I just don't want any media exposure, that's all. Look, come on to the back and have a cup of coffee. Unless you brought that champagne?"

He snapped his fingers. "Forgot. Of course, this is kind of early in the day. If I'd realized things would be so festive here. . . . When do the mariachis start playing?"

"All right, all right." She led the way to the back of the shop. The rear view could never be as good as the head-on one, but she held his interest.

When they were seated in two of the black leather chairs, he said, "What have you been doing with yourself these two weeks?"

"I've been very busy getting ready to open. You know, dusting books, pricing books." She stopped abruptly. Stu had the feeling there was a third item in the series she had decided to censor. Something was bothering this girl. And it was his duty to brother Rodney to find out what it was.

She went on, "And of course I have had some business since I opened, even without media coverage."

"Where are you living?" he inquired casually.

"Upstairs. Uncle Oscar set up an apartment up there."

39

"That must be lonely, all by yourself. A little scary even."

"No, I've been fine," she said unconcernedly. "I've been protected by the ghosts."

"Ghosts?"

"I'm teasing, I'm teasing. I've just always been an independent sort. Rod could tell you that."

Actually, Stu reflected, that was what he'd tried to tell Rodney. An independent modern woman wouldn't need or want a local watchdog checking up on her all the time. But now that he was face to face with her independence, he found it oddly disquieting. Still, she had asked his help.

"I've made a number of friends," she said. "The mail carrier is very nice. And some of my fellow merchants have been very helpful. I haven't been a hermit."

"Of course not. I'm intrigued by these signed books."

She darted over the rolltop desk and brought him a stack of half a dozen. He looked at the spines.

"Hm. Scott Fitzgerald, Nathanael West, James M. Cain, Aldous Huxley, Craig Rice, Horace McCoy, Frank Gruber. An interesting assortment. And they're all presentation copies?"

"Not presentations, just autographed. Just the name signed in each case."

"And you want to know if the signatures are genuine?"

"Yes. I'd like someone who knows those signatures to look at them and give an opinion of their authenticity. And I'd rather not have it known the books came from this shop. I don't mean I want some kind of heavy scientific analysis by a graphologist. Just a good visual inspection by someone familiar with the signatures or who has them to compare."

Stu nodded. "Okay. I can provide that this afternoon, I think. Get them back to you tonight. I doubt that you have to worry, though. I mean, Frank Gruber was quite a writer, but I don't really think anybody would go to the trouble of forging his signature on a book, do you?"

She shrugged. "Uncle Oscar always said that funny things happen in the book business."

Stu downed his coffee. "Well, look, why don't I just carry these off now, so I can get them back to you this evening. How long are you staying open?"

"I'm really not sure," she said. "As long as business stays this brisk, I guess."

"Right. Don't let it rattle you. Just make them form a line." He really liked this woman.

On the way to the front of the store, he glanced at some of the titles on the shelves. He liked old bookstores, always had. "Here's a nice one," he said. *The Face of the Man From Saturn.* You like s.f.?"

"Once in a while," she said. "Who wrote it?"

"Fellow named Harry Stephen Keeler." He opened the front cover. "This one's signed, too. John Hancock size."

"My uncle used to joke about him. He signed a lot of books in his time. Uncle Oscar sometimes claimed there were more signed Keelers than unsigned ones."

"Wouldn't you like this one authenticated, too?"

"No," she said. "I'm not worried about that one."

"Okay."

She watched him walk to his car, giving her a friendly wave before climbing in. He was a nice fellow, not much like Rod at all. Over the phone, he'd seemed somewhat overpowering and exhausting, but in person, the effect dissipated. His face seemed to soften his relentless facetiousness, and for all his frantic speech, he seemed basically relaxed. She thought she could trust him and had a feeling that she would be telling him the whole fantastic story that evening. She had to tell somebody. She was proud of, or at least resigned to, her loner status, her independence. But some matters just cried out for discussion.

As the afternoon wore on, a few more customers came and went. A few even bought. Only one was memorable.

At about three-thirty, a red Mercedes pulled up in front of the shop, and a white-haired, distinguished-looking man of indeterminate middle age stepped out. Rachel knew he looked familiar, probably from a dust jacket rather than life. He had that dust-jackety look about him. She tried to picture him with a pipe and a dog.

He looked in the window rather casually, then spotted her sitting at the front desk. She realized immediately that seeing her was causing more of a gleam in his eye than any of the exhibited first editions. He entered the store.

"Miss Hennings, I believe," he said with a slight bow.

"Yes," she said. "I have the feeling I should know you."

"No, no, we've never met. If we had, I'm sure I would remember. My name is Arlen Kitchener."

He obviously expected the same kind of thunderous response as if he'd said Frank Sinatra or John Travolta or Pope John Paul.

Rachel merely raised an eyebrow. "Of course," she said. "I knew your face was familiar." She had never read one of his books.

"I was a good friend of your uncle, and when I heard you were reopening the shop, I thought I should stop by and say hello."

Rachel knew the first part of that was a gross exaggeration, but the second part made her more curious. "How did you find out I had reopened?"

"Edgar Ferris is my attorney."

"Oh."

"He had told me you were a charming young woman, but nothing he said could possibly have prepared me . . ." He saw his words were having the opposite of their desired effect, so he quickly shifted gears. "Tell me, then. Can I do anything to help you out? I'd be more than glad to have an autographing party when my new book comes out."

The idea seemed to panic her slightly. "Uh, no, thank you, Mr. Kitchener. You're very kind, but I don't think it will be necessary. I don't plan to deal in new books, and I don't want to change the basic nature of the store. It's always been a quiet sort of place, a refuge, and—"

"Oscar could afford to keep it that way," said Arlen Kitchener, cooling slightly.

"I don't mean to offend you."

"Not at all, not at all. I respect your wishes, of course. We don't want Vermilion's to suffer from any pushy commercialism."

Arlen cast his eyes idly along the shelves and quickly spotted several book club editions of his own novels.

"Well, the least I can do is sign those books of mine you have now, eh? That should do something for their value."

"Thank you," said Rachel, "you're very kind."

Arlen took the books down and began signing them with a quick stroke of the ballpoint. "Always be on the lookout for signed or inscribed copies," he said. "Get as many as you can. It will do wonders for your business."

"Oh, I know that," said Rachel.

Arlen searched her face with his eyes. Her face was solemn as can be, but he had the odd feeling she was laughing at him, having a private joke with herself. Other people's humor had never been his strong point, nor was his own humor.

He passed the books to her across the counter. "There we are. I think, if I may make a suggestion, you might want to up the price on those slightly. They should bring more than a dollar each now, eh?"

"Thank you very much, Mr. Kitchener. I truly appreciate your interest."

"If I can help further, please call on me. Now I have to go. I will be back."

With a smile, he turned and left, returning to his Mercedes. Her cool beauty would bring him back all right. She was an odd girl, a puzzle to be solved. She was so unimpressed with a famous novelist walking into her shop. And she seemed to have inherited Oscar Vermilion's anti-commercial bias without, he knew very well, inheriting his millions as well. A very unusual young lady.

Rachel watched him go, thinking what a very strange man he was. She returned the books to the one-dollar shelf. It was a long-standing policy of Vermilion's never to change prices upward.

One other thing occurred to her. That bearded customer who had come to the shop looking lost and baffled often stopped and looked at those Kitchener titles. Never bought them, but always looked at them pensively.

5.

Stu returned to the shop at seven o'clock, the stack of autographed books under his arm. The OPEN sign was still in the door, but Rachel was nowhere in sight.

Putting the books down, he waited a moment, then shouted in a voice as different from his own as he could make it, "Hey, goddam it, where are your self-help books?"

"Just a minute," came Rachel's voice from the back of the store.

"I need a book on how to control my temper, and if I don't get one soon, I'm gonna tear this joint apart."

"They don't work that fast, Stu," the voice called. A moment later she appeared.

"Hey, you are psychic. How'd you know it was me?"

She smiled. "I was upstairs changing. I saw you drive up through the window."

"I'm sorry I drove up through the window," he said. "You can take the cost out of my consulting fee."

She had indeed been changing. While it would not be quite accurate to say she had dressed up, she had put on a skirt and sweater, and the effect was dazzling. She turned the sign in the door to the CLOSED side, locked the door, and pulled the shade. Stu found the actions curiously alarming.

"Have you eaten?" she asked.

"No, I've been too busy checking out autographs . . ."

"Good. Come on upstairs and I'll give you dinner. It's the least I can do."

"Great, but don't you want to know . . ."

"Oh, yes, the verdict. They are real, aren't they?"

"Every single signature is genuine. The guy I took them to is an autograph dealer in Beverly Hills. He was really impressed. You don't see some of these signatures too often, he said. He wondered where all the books came from. I told him I didn't know."

She nodded. "My story, I think, will be that a wealthy local collector has fallen on hard times, is selling off his collection little

44

by little, and does not want to be identified. I have to do something to explain this influx of signed editions."

"But it's not true, right?"

"Not true?"

"The way you said that, it sounded like that was a story you'd made up. Am I wrong?"

"No, you're right, Stu. I'm going to tell you the whole thing. I badly need advice. What I'm going to tell you will be very hard to believe. In fact, there's no way in the world you're going to believe me."

"You don't look like a congenital liar."

"You say that now, but wait till you hear. Maybe I can demonstrate for you. Then you'll know exactly the situation I'm in, and you'll be in a better position to advise me. It will help if your first advice is *not* that I see a psychiatrist."

"I know a psychology professor in Arizona who'd work cheap." She smiled. "Rod would never understand this, believe me. He'd be no help. But you might."

"You're making me curious, Rachel."

"So I'll know you'll stay."

"I'll stay as long as you want me to stay. I'll even stay *longer* than you want me to stay. I've already stayed longer than Rod wants me to stay."

"Rod isn't here."

"Oh, yes, he is. I can feel him watching me. Ever had that feeling?"

"You have no idea."

"So what are you going to demonstrate? I'm expiring of curiosity."

"Shall we eat first?"

"I changed my mind. I'm expiring of hunger."

They went upstairs to her apartment where they shared a steak, a salad, and a bottle of wine. Actual home cooking. Why had Stu been expecting Col. Sanders? Rachel laughed a lot and talked a lot. It was partly the wine but mostly the relief she felt at the prospect of talking to someone else about what was going on.

"Seriously now," he asked. "How much business are you doing?"

"Oh, you'd be surprised. I wouldn't say the shop is on a paying basis just yet, but I get a lot of interesting customers. Sometimes it seems like there are more sellers than buyers, though."

"You mean people who want to sell you their libraries?"

"It's something you don't have to deal with in the new book business and it takes a lot of tact. I haven't bought many books in the past week, but I've had my opportunities, yes, indeed."

"Anything good?"

"Not really. Sellers seem to come in several categories. First there are the ones with boxes full of book club editions. Nice to read but too plentiful to be worth anything. I tell them to donate them to their local library instead, even though I know most libraries would be no gladder to see them than I am. Then you've got the magazine subscribers cleaning out their accumulated *Sunset* and *Sports Illustrated* and *National Geographic* runs for the last ten years or so. They're astonished to know a book dealer has no use for their wares, even when I explain that I don't deal in back issue magazines. Then they want me to take them off their hands for nothing, and when I won't do even that they're really hurt. Oh, you have to be ruthless in this business, Stu."

"I wouldn't have dreamed you had it in you. Does this mean you don't want to make an offer on my old issues of *Playboy* and *Penthouse*?"

"Now those might be worth something, but I'm not sure I want them around."

"I wish my editor would let me sell you some review copies."

"Now there's another category I can tell you about: the book reviewers who somehow expect a handsome price for boxes full of bright and shiny new copies of unknown fiction that sank without a ripple on publication five years ago."

"So much for the review copies. But doesn't anybody ever bring in a valuable old heirloom that's worth a fortune?"

"They seem to think so. The attic cleaners think any book with a nineteenth-century imprint, regardless of poor condition or reprint status, simply must be worth a lot of money. And of course most of them aren't."

"Isn't there anybody with something worthwhile to peddle?"

46

"Not enough to make a category worth talking about."

"Where did these signed copies come from?"

Rachel smiled. "Stu, you have no idea what a large question that is."

At about nine o'clock, she brought Stu back downstairs, seated him in one of the black leather chairs, and took several books out of a little box near the rolltop desk. She took a fountain pen out of the drawer, placed the books on the coffee table between them, and sat down.

She smiled self-consciously. "I don't even know if this will work with an audience. But if you can see it, at least you won't think I'm insane."

"I won't think that," Stu assured her. "I mean, Rod would have told me if you were crazy. A psychologist should know, right?"

She took a breath, and the smile disappeared. "These are some books Uncle Oscar apparently acquired just before he died. He hadn't processed or priced them yet."

She opened the cover of the first book. Stu saw that it was a copy of Erle Stanley Gardner's *The Court of Last Resort*. With a spasmodic gesture, she grasped the pen, then seemingly without looking at the book wrote a name on the flyleaf. Stu arched his head forward to see what she was writing.

ERLE STANLEY GARDNER

Stu didn't say anything and neither did she. She simply went on to the next book. In a completely different hand, she wrote a name on the flyleaf, this time a name Stu was unfamiliar with.

On the third book, she put the pen in her left hand and signed a third completely dissimilar signature.

In a matter of a couple of minutes, she had signed six books in this way.

She closed the last one, sighed, yawned, looked at the ceiling for a few moments with her eyes closed, and then looked back at Stu. His eyes were wide and staring.

She smiled slightly. "Well?"

"That was quite a demonstration," said Stu. "Quite a demonstration. How did you learn to do that?"

"I didn't. It just happens. I hardly know what the pen is doing.

It just skips along the pages and comes up with the signature. It works with either hand, depending I assume on whether the author was right-handed or left-handed."

"Are you normally ambidextrous?"

"Not a bit."

"And those books you had me check out. Were they . . . ?"

She nodded her head slowly. "I think you can see why I couldn't keep this to myself. I had to tell somebody."

Stu's mind was working fast, advancing and discarding theories. "And you claim you don't do that consciously?"

She scowled slightly. "That's just what I 'claim,' " she said, emphasizing the last word. "And it's true."

"Okay. Are you in some kind of a trance when you do it?"

"I don't think you'd call it a trance. I'm awake and aware of what's going on. But the signatures come out the same whether I look at the page while I'm doing it or not. It's as if someone else is doing it. I'm just the tool. And of course that's true."

Stu swallowed. "Of course." For a minute he said nothing more. He thought over the names of the writers whose signatures he'd had authenticated, the names of the ones he'd seen go on paper tonight. "Are all the authors involved, uh . . ."

"Dead? Yes, they're all dead. I suppose they'd have to be."

"They would? You couldn't have learned the signatures of living writers?"

"Stu, I told you I didn't *learn* anything. It just happens."

"Yes, yes, I understand that. But obviously you did see those signatures and learn them at some time, subconsciously, even if you don't remember. And now, your subconscious is reproducing them on the page. It's weird, I'll agree, but it's the only feasible explanation. It's a form of self-hypnosis, I guess."

"I've never seen most of these signatures before in my life."

"Sure, sure, that you *remember*. But you have seen them. You must have. Didn't Rod tell me you were an artist?"

"Not an artist exactly. I do have some small talent, and I do draw and paint."

"I understand." Stu got up from his chair with the idea of pacing the floor, but the small floor space of the back of the bookshop didn't give him a great deal of room. "You have this artistic ability. And that, combined with the mental images you made of these authors' signatures at some time in the past, enables you to reproduce them, without even knowing you're doing it on a conscious level. To put it bluntly, you have an extraordinary talent for forgery."

"I'm not a forger," she said in an even voice. She was feeling irritation and anger and trying to hold them down. After all, she told herself, he was reacting quite naturally. What rational person wouldn't look for that kind of an explanation when confronted with something like this?

"Hey, don't get me wrong. I'm not saying you're any kind of a criminal."

"Thank you."

"But it's the only explanation that makes sense."

"This very afternoon, you were told by an expert that these signatures are real."

"Of course. But it was only a visual examination. He didn't look at them under a magnifying glass, or do a study of the ink, or do whatever they do to decide whether a signature is real or not. He just looked at them, compared them with other examples he had or had seen, and concluded that they were very likely genuine."

"They *are* genuine."

"But . . ." Stu allowed himself to drop back into the black leather chair, as if drained. "Okay, okay. You have my theory. Let's hear yours."

"All right. What this is is a form of automatic writing. It's something I've had brushes with before, though I was not sure of it at the time. Since these signatures started happening, I've been reading up on the subject. Some of the recorded examples make this look commonplace by comparison. There's an Englishwoman named Rosemary Brown who has had music dictated to her by dead composers like Liszt, Beethoven, Chopin, Bach, and Brahms. And she has no musical training to speak of, either. The music she's produced is far beyond her capabilities."

"Rachel, anybody in the newspaper business knows about the weird stories that come out of England."

"I don't know why I'm telling you this!" She was getting mad. She couldn't help it. "There's a whole book about that case. You should read it. You could also read about the woman in St. Louis who had several books dictated to her by a seventeenth-century woman. And—"

"Don't give me that crap, Rachel. There's a lot of ridiculous stuff written in books. Conan Doyle thought he saw pictures of fairies in the garden. I've seen the pictures, and it's a damned obvious example of trick photography."

"We're not talking about fairies, and this isn't a case of trick photography! You won't discuss this seriously because you're blinded by prejudice."

"Let's see now," said Stu, in a lowered voice. "All these dead authors are lining up behind your chair to come and sign their books using your hand. Literary people are rarely that easy to regiment, Rachel. It's hard for me to see Huxley and Fitzgerald and Gardner and Chandler lining up like that to sign your books. You must have one hell of a 'control.' Is it the traditional Indian or what? Whoever he is, he's an organizational genius. If he were a social director on a cruise ship, he'd have everybody playing shuffleboard in the first hour."

She'd been right the first time, Rachel thought. His conversational style was tiresome and offensive. But who would understand this if he wouldn't? Rod would have come up with the same sort of explanation, but he would have known more jargon and been able to make it sound more plausible. But she knew the truth.

"You're frightened," she said. "I guess that's understandable, but it's not an excuse for being—"

"Frightened?" Stu's dormant macho pride came to the fore now. "The only thing that frightens me is that you're either out of your mind or conning me."

"Conning you?" she said unbelievingly.

"Sure, conning me. What a piece of misdirection. Houdini would be proud. I saw you sign those books tonight in six different hands, but I don't have the slightest idea what those writers' signatures look like. You're probably artist enough to do six different handwritings, especially when you can bring your left hand on in relief. And as for the ones I checked out, sure, they're genuine. But I only have your word for it that you signed those. You almost sucked me in, baby. Now what is it you want? Do you expect to get money out of me in some kind of pigeon drop or do you want to get your name in the paper or what?"

"You'd better keep my name *out* of the paper," she said shrilly, "or I'll—I'll sue you, that's what I'll do. And the only pigeon drop is going to be on your head the next time you . . ." She trailed off. It had sounded like a snappy retort, but she didn't know how to finish it. "I think you'd better leave."

"I think I had," he said. "I don't want us to disturb your neighbors in the disco across the street. Good night, and thanks for the nice dinner."

After some fumbling with the door lock that aggravated him no end, he was off in a shower of jingles.

Listening to the last faint ring of the bell fade away, Rachel sat back down and shook her head. That obviously hadn't been too good an idea. But she'd needed to share this thing with someone, and who else could she tell?

She briefly felt completely alone, as if she'd lost her last hope of help. She felt an exasperating tightness in her throat. No, she told herself fiercely, I am not going to sit here and cry because Stu Wellman isn't the sympathetic friend I'd hoped he would be. It's just ridiculous, and I never cry without a good reason.

She certainly didn't feel like sleeping, though she could have used some sleep, so she went to the rolltop desk determined to price the few items remaining from Uncle Oscar's last big purchase. The signed copies she put aside. She still couldn't quite bring herself to sell them. She didn't think of herself as a forger, she knew the signatures were genuine, and yet she couldn't offer them for sale as such. Not quite yet.

She marked prices in pencil, slightly higher than Oscar Vermilion had been charging, but still quite reasonable. The last one in the box was by the man who had visited the store today, Arlen Kitchener. She vaguely remembered Uncle Oscar mentioning Kitchener. He hadn't liked him very much. The book was called *The Atlantis Courier.*

Dust jacket, nice condition. She turned to the verso of the title page. First printing, too. Not an uncommon item, though. Three dollars seemed about right to her. She turned back to the front

51

endpaper. Her pencil wavered in the upper right hand corner, though, and seemed to shoot down, uninvited, to the middle of the page.

In an instant she thought, No, this isn't right, living authors can't do this.

The pencil wrote,

RANSOM BLAISDELL

Ransom Blaisdell? Who was Ransom Blaisdell?

6. When she awoke the next morning, following another fitful night's sleep, Rachel's first impulse was to call Stu Wellman and ask him what he knew about a person named Ransom Blaisdell, who may have been a writer. But no, she decided, Stu had been too rude the night before. She thought he had been understandably scared of the unknown and this had made him act in an unaccustomed way. Also, she fully expected an apologetic call from him, maybe today and maybe next week. But in any case, it was up to him to make the first move.

Instead, after having breakfast and going downstairs to open the shop, she turned back to what she believed would be the next best source of literary information, the public library.

Reaching the reference desk after a few minutes on hold, she said, "Do you have any information on—"

"Automatic writing," said a pleasant male voice.

"What?" she said, somewhat startled.

"Automatic writing. I recognized your voice. You asked for books on automatic writing."

"Oh, yes."

"Did you get what you needed?"

"You were very helpful. This time I want to know what you have on a writer named Ransom Blaisdell."

"Do you know if he's living?"

"I'm not sure, but I suspect not," she said. "All I can tell you is that he probably lived in the Los Angeles area or worked here at some time in the last forty or fifty years."

"Okay. Hold on." After a few minutes, the voice returned. "Found him. He's only listed in one source, *Contemporary Authors*. Born in Los Angeles in 1931. His father was a screenwriter, his mother a starlet who retired from pictures when he was a kid. Graduated from UCLA in 1951, free-lance writer ever since. From his biography here, he's never held any other job. As for his writing, he seems to have written anything and everything, no particular specialty. He wrote many paperback originals: mysteries, westerns, science fiction, pornography—"

"Pornography?"

"Yes, he seems to have been quite proud of his porno novels, lists a whole bunch right along with his regular stuff. Most of them were published under other names, though. He also seems to have done a lot of how-to books, self-help stuff, books exploiting various fads. Karate, hula hoop, hot tubs. Almost always paperbacks. He lists a bunch of magazines he contributed to, quite a range. He also apparently wrote a bit for TV, and one hardcover novel under his own name. He collaborated on a number of celebrity autobiographies. In our catalogue we have his novel listed, a book called *A Hard Course,* published in 1963, also a few of his 'as told to' jobs, the celebrity bios. None of the paperbacks. That's just a summary. Was there a particular title you were interested in?"

"No, no particular title. You say he *is* still alive?"

"As far as I can tell. He was at the time this volume of *Contemporary Authors* came out, and it's one of the latest ones. If you like, I could check the L.A. *Times* index and see if there's been an obituary."

"No, that's all right. Does the biography give an address by any chance?"

"Oh, yes. It gives his agent's address, fellow named Clarence Gustavson, and it also gives a home address in Sherman Oaks."

"Let me have those." The librarian read them off and she wrote them down. "Does it have a telephone number?"

"No, but I can—"

"That's all right. I have some phone books here. Thank you very much. You've been most helpful."

"You have a lovely speaking voice over the phone."

"Thank you." She hung up as quickly as graciousness allowed.

Rachel quickly found Ransom Blaisdell's home phone number in one of the several volumes covering the Los Angeles area. She hesitated a moment, though, before dialing.

Why am I calling this man? Oh, I know why I'm calling. I want to know if he's alive and if so what he's doing signing another man's book. But I can't say that.

After a moment's thought, she dialed the number.

A tired-sounding female voice answered. "Hello."

"Hello, is this Mrs. Blaisdell?"

"Yes, it is."

"My name is Rachel Hennings, of Vermilion's Bookshop in Los Angeles. I was wondering if your husband is at home."

There was a slight pause. "I'm sorry, Miss Hennings. My husband is dead."

"Oh, I am sorry. Did he die recently?"

"About three months ago."

"How dreadful. That's about the same time my Uncle Oscar died."

"Oscar Vermilion?"

"Yes, I believe he was a friend of your husband's. That was why I called. I'm trying to let my uncle's old customers know that the shop is open for business again. And while I know it can't be the kind of gathering place it was, I want them to know they're all welcome. Oh, I'm sorry. This must be painful for you."

"Oh, it's all right", said the woman. "Yes, my husband did frequently visit Vermilion's. It was one of his favorite places. He said Mr. Vermilion really understood writers and knew literature. Randy said that even if he couldn't write literature, he liked to talk about it now and then." There was a faint note of bitterness in her voice.

Rachel was mentally improvising. There was no logical reason for continuing this conversation much further, but she felt there must be some way to get a little more information.

"Well, I hardly think my uncle would agree that your husband wasn't writing literature, Mrs. Blaisdell."

"Oh, I think he would."

Yes, perhaps he would. "Arlen Kitchener dropped by the store yesterday."

Another pause, as well there might be. Rachel hadn't been exactly deft in her manner of bringing Kitchener's name into the conversation.

"Oh?" said Mrs. Blaisdell. "I don't know him. I know his name, of course."

"Well, I really mustn't take any more of your time, Mrs. Blaisdell. I'm sorry to bother you, and I offer my condolences on your husband's death. Did he die quite suddenly?"

"You could say quite suddenly, yes. My husband was murdered."

"Oh, I am sorry, you must think I'm terrible, calling you like this and opening up old wounds and . . . well, you must accept my apology. And, if there is anything I can do for you, just let me know. I feel a sense of friendship for all the old Vermilion customers, and . . . well, you understand what I mean."

"Thank you very much."

"Uh, yes, good-bye."

Hanging up, Rachel shook herself. What must that woman have thought of me, babbling like an idiot? I didn't sound like myself at all. And she must have realized she was just being grilled for information.

That's it, Rachel told herself. No more poking your nose in anything but old books. Leave the snooping to Nancy Drew. Who never became involved in murder. Mysteries, yes, but never murder.

Ghosts hovering around the bookshop couldn't scare Rachel. And neither could bookish burglars. But murder could.

That afternoon, the signed book club editions by Arlen Kitchener sold. The buyer seemed very happy to get them at a dollar a throw and asked if there were any more signed Kitcheners around. Rachel said no. She was tempted to say, "Not exactly," and show the collector the copy of *The Atlantis Courier*, but she resisted the temptation.

Another customer that same afternoon was the bearded man who had been in the store twice the week before. Again, he seemed nervous and spent an inordinate amount of time browsing in widely divergent areas of the store. As before, he made Rachel wonder what he was up to, though again he didn't really seem particularly menacing to her.

Finally, he drifted back to the rolltop desk where the books she had signed the night before were still sitting. She walked to the back of the store to tell him that the books there weren't processed yet and were not for sale. He had opened one of the books and slammed it shut when she approached. She couldn't tell which one it was.

"I'm sorry, the books on the desk aren't ready for sale yet."

"Uh . . . gosh, that's too bad." His eyes seemed to light on the copy of *The Court of Last Resort*. "I'm a Gardner fan," he said. He opened the front cover. "Signed. Wow. You don't see that many signed Gardners, even though he lived out here. Won't you sell me this? I'll pay what it's worth."

"Well, I really couldn't do that. I don't really know if that's a genuine signature. It could be a forgery."

"Oh, no, it's a real signature. I've seen one before."

Rachel almost quoted him a price, but someting stopped her. "No, I'm afraid not," she said. "I'm sorry."

The bearded man shrugged. "When *will* these be on sale?"

"I don't really know. Was there another one you were interested in?"

"Oh, no, just the Gardner. Well, so long. Thanks."

The bearded man left the store. He was certainly an odd one. Was the Kitchener the other book he'd been looking at? The works of Kitchener had seemed to interest him before, though he'd never bought any. Oh, well, book lovers were odd people.

So she had had a chance to sell one of her "ghost" books and passed it up. It was silly probably. They were meant to be sold, certainly, to help the store. Weren't they?

At five o'clock, a sheepish-looking Stu Wellman appeared at her door. He was holding a paper bag with what looked like a bottle in it.

"I never delivered on that bottle of champagne I was supposed to come up with," he said.

"Thank you," she said simply. "But we had no—"

"No, we never signed a contract, I'll agree. Look, that wasn't me that was here last night. I never act quite so stupid, at least not in that way. And I don't accuse people of things without knowing all the facts. My journalistic training and ingrained objectivity forbid that."

"So that was an imposter?"

"Yes. It was. A rampant idiot who occasionally uses my name. And face. You have no idea how embarrassing it can be sometimes. Anyway, I was hoping you'd have dinner with me tonight. And maybe we can talk about your problem. That is, not that you have a problem."

57

She laughed. "I'm not sure if I do or not. Do you know the name Ransom Blaisdell?"

He squinted at her. "Yes I do. Writer. He was murdered."

"Do you know anything else?"

Stu hesitated. "It sounds like a sick joke."

"What do you mean?"

"Just that when he was alive he was a professional ghost-writer."

"You aren't putting me on?"

"Why should I? I've sworn off snappy patter."

She took the bagged bottle. "I'll just run this upstairs to the refrigerator. We can share it on some festive occasion."

"Not now?"

"No, it's not exactly festive now."

"Are you going to go to dinner with me?"

"Sure. As soon as I can close up the store."

"Thank God you haven't established any regular hours."

"I'll have to sometime. But, Stu, before we eat, can we find out any more about Ransom Blaisdell? His death and so forth?"

"I can get us into the morgue over at the *News-Canvas*. It's after-hours, but . . ."

"Good. I'll be ready in ten minutes. Make yourself at home." She rushed toward the stairs at the back of the store.

Stu browsed rather aimlessly in the psychology section.

The newspaper morgue after-hours, long rows of filing cabinets casting weird shadows on the wall, struck Rachel as far more macabre than her bookstore, though she had no way of knowing if it was as widely inhabited. What ghost would want to spend his or her time in a place like this?

"We have to be sure to keep everything the way we left it," said Stu. "Marion the librarian gets very upset."

"Is her name really Marion or do you just call her that?"

"It's a guy, and his name really is Marion. He's not really a librarian, though; he's a burned-out reporter. Anyway, he doesn't really like anybody in here at night, but the night editor insists that these files be available."

Lighting up one corner of the room, Stu pulled out the file on Ransom Blaisdell.

"I'm surprised this isn't all computerized," she said.

"Then you'd *never* be able to find anything."

The newspaper files on Ransom Blaisdell filled in a few details to supplement what they already knew. The articles made clear that in the last few years of his life, most of Blaisdell's income was from ghosting books for other writers. Since one of the prime features of any ghostwriting contract was secrecy, none of Blaisdell's assignments in that line had been identified, except for those in which he had received credit on the book, as a "with" or an "as told to." Sometimes, in the case of vainer celebrities, his name would not appear on the cover or title page at all, but a short acknowledgement thanking him for his help in preparing the manuscript would tip off those in the know that he was the actual author.

"He was a versatile ghost," said Stu. "Movie stars, business moguls, even a few athletes. Candy Helms, the tennis player."

"Stu, I guess everybody knows that celebrities who publish their memoirs usually have a professional to do the actual writing for them. But why would a real writer use a ghost?"

Stu shrugged. "Sometimes they get lazy and tired of writing, but their name value on a book is so great neither they nor their agents or publishers can afford to let the potential sales vanish. So they bring in a ghost, who gets a tidy sum in exchange for writing the book and not telling anybody. It happens more than you'd think, especially with commercial writers of long, successful series. Also, some writers will take on more projects than they can handle themselves so they start to panic when two or three different deadlines start to come close and they call in a ghost to bail them out. Sometimes writers just lose their action—it happens to athletes and musicians, too. One day, they're blocked, can't write anymore. Whatever the reason is, there's always plenty of work for a good, discreet ghostwriter. And that's what Ransom Blaisdell was."

"I wonder if his ghostwriting had anything to do with his death," Rachel mused.

"I'm sure the police looked into all the angles."

Ransom Blaisdell had died on March 15. His body was found in his Sherman Oaks living room by his wife, who had just returned from a shopping trip. The police discovered he had been killed by a blow from a "blunt instrument," specifically a bowling trophy on his mantle.

"That's only five days after Uncle Oscar died," Rachel said.

Stu looked at her. "You don't think there's a connection, do you?"

She shrugged. "I don't know. Maybe."

"I'm sure there was nothing funny about your uncle's death. His heart just gave out."

"Oh, I'm sure you're right. I *hope* you're right. I'd hate to think that Uncle Oscar was . . . but there's no reason to think that."

If the *News-Canvas* reports were accurate, the police hadn't got very far toward solving the murder of Ransom Blaisdell. There had been two coffee cups on the table in the living room, indicating that Blaisdell had been entertaining a visitor while his wife was gone, suggesting that the probable killer was known to Blaisdell and didn't seem to represent a real threat to him. A strange car had been seen parked in the neighborhood around the probable time of the crime, but the woman who saw it unfortunately knew nothing about cars. All that could be established was that it was a late-model compact, light green in color. The pursuit of that car had given the police a great deal to do among Blaisdell's acquaintances, but nothing had come of it.

Among the persons being interviewed by the police, aside from his wife Estelle and their neighbors, were a close friend of the family, Marvin Fodor, and the late writer's agent, Clarence Gustavson. Lieutenant Milo Corning was identified as heading the LAPD investigation.

"Marvin Fodor," Rachel said slowly.

"Do you know him?"

"Is there a picture of him anywhere here?"

"No. It wasn't that big a story that we've got a picture of everybody mentioned. Do you know him?"

"I have a feeling I should. There's something in the back of my mind, but I can't quite bring it out. Maybe I'll think of it later."

The story had stayed in the news for several days but soon petered out. No major literary names were ever mentioned in connection with the crime, and no real leads seemed to have come to light.

After about half an hour with the clippings about Blaisdell, Stu said, "Had enough? I don't know about you, but I'm getting hungry."

"Oh, okay," said Rachel. She seemed remote and distracted. "I guess that's all we can find out here, huh?"

"Are you going to tell me what's going on? Why is this murder so interesting to you?"

"I don't want to get involved in murder, Stu, I really don't. But I may not have any choice."

"I don't understand."

"I'll tell you the whole story when we've eaten. But for now, I think I know one of the books that Ransom Blaisdell ghosted. A best-seller. Would that make a good item for your column?"

"Suddenly you're thinking publicity?"

"Oh, not for me. My name has to stay out of it."

"Do you have proof?"

"Proof enough for me. But not for anybody else. I think one of the books Ransom Blaisdell ghosted was *The Atlantis Courier*."

"You're kidding. I've never heard any suggestion that Arlen Kitchener used ghostwriters."

"You've heard one now."

"How do you know this?"

"Ransom Blaisdell told me."

7. Sarah Kitchener was used to the sound of typewriter keys. When they stopped, which was seldom, it made her nervous, and she would get up from her chair in the living room and have a look in Arlen's study, half fearing he had had a heart attack and slumped over the typewriter. From time to time, he had to stop and think, but if he thought for more than thirty seconds at a time, he was thinking too much. He often said you did your thinking before you started. If you tried to think in mid-manuscript, he said, it was like a shortstop trying to think when the ball was coming at him. Thinking made error. Thinking ruined the reflexes.

Tonight Arlen was clacking away, two hundred words per minute on the average, and giving her little to worry about. She was a worrier, and that was that. So she worried about Craig, their son. He seemed to have such a chip on his shoulder with his father, and it hadn't always been that way. Ten or twelve years ago, at the tail end of the tumultuous sixties when Craig had been an activist junior high school student, the two of them had argued for hours on end, but there was no rancor in it. Now, it was as though they genuinely disliked each other. And when they argued, they seemed to be trying to hurt each other, not just to score debating points. What was worse, she had the feeling that they probably moderated their quarrels when she was around and were even more heated and cruel when she wasn't there.

A couple of weeks ago, they'd had some kind of confrontation while she was out. When she'd returned home, they had announced that Craig would be moving out of the house, something she had always felt would be a good idea but that they both seemed to resist. Craig had said he'd be out as soon as he found a suitable place. But he was still here, and Sarah had the feeling he was never going.

Whatever Sarah did these evenings, she did quietly. Knitting, crocheting, reading. Any noise, of TV or radio or even of music on the stereo, was verboten when Arlen was working. According to long-standing family tradition, she would bring him a cup of hot

62

chocolate promptly at ten o'clock, and he would stop typing, even in mid-sentence sometimes, and they would talk for a while. Though these days they seemed to have little to talk about, the ritual continued. In earlier years, Craig would join them when he was home, but now Craig stayed out consistently, as much, she often thought, to avoid that ten o'clock ritual as for any other reason.

Unusually fidgety tonight, she picked up the morning paper's television logs and glanced at the offerings on Channel 28, the local PBS outlet. If there was anything really good on, she could always go up to their bedroom and watch it. She wouldn't disturb Arlen that way. But there was nothing that attractive.

She looked at the clock, silently ticking. Nine-thirty.

The telephone rang. It was a muted ring, the volume turned way down so as not to disturb Arlen. She picked it up.

"Hello."

"Mr. Kitchener, please." The voice was a raspy whisper.

"I'm sorry. My husband is working at the moment. May I take a message?"

"I'm sure he'd want to talk to me."

"He never takes calls while he's working, I'm sorry. Whom shall I say called?"

"Ransom Blaisdell."

"Who? But. . . . Is this some kind of prank? Ransom Blaisdell is dead."

"I'll call again. Good-bye."

Replacing the receiver, Sarah wondered if she should say anything to Arlen. Not now, of course, but when she brought his hot chocolate. It was some kind of crank call, scarcely worth mentioning, but probably he'd want to know about it.

The possibility didn't occur to her then that the police might want to know about it, too.

Arlen was far more upset than she would have expected. He tried to pick up his cup of chocolate and it rattled in the saucer, spilling some. He placed it back on the table. Sarah didn't think of her husband as a nervous man, but this seemed to make one of him.

"If he calls again, I want to talk to him."

"It's just a joke, Arlen. It has to be."

"It's someone trying to frighten me."

"But why? It's a little scary to get a call from a man who is supposed to be dead, but I don't see why it makes you react this way."

Arlen smiled weakly. "I don't mean to alarm you, dear. But Blaisdell was murdered. So naturally, this kind of thing is a little disturbing. Don't you worry about it."

I wasn't until now, she wanted to say. There was something Arlen wasn't telling her, she realized, and he wasn't about to.

As they finished their chocolate in silence, they heard the front door opening. Arlen Kitchener jumped a foot.

Their son Craig appeared in the doorway.

"Hi," he said.

"You're home early, dear," said his mother, pleased at the idea. "Will you have a cup of chocolate?"

"No, thanks," he said, coming and taking a chair in the study.

He sat for a moment as if waiting for something. Then he looked sharply at his father and said, "You look like you've seen a ghost, dad."

"I'm just amazed to see you home before midnight."

"I've long since reached the age of majority, dad. You can't ground me."

"I can throw you out," Arlen returned, but somewhat absently, his heart not in it.

"You two wear me out!" Sarah snapped. "We had a kind of unusual phone call this evening, Craig. Someone who said he was Ransom Blaisdell."

"Ransom Blaisdell? The guy who was murdered?"

"It's some stupid prank," said Arlen. "Not worth talking about. When he calls again, I'll talk to him and tell him where to get off."

"If it's some stupid prank, what makes you so sure he'll call again?"

"I don't know. If he calls again." Arlen, his hand steadier now, drained his cup. "I really ought to get back to work. Thank you, my dear."

Sarah stood up. Their son stayed sprawled in his chair and said, "You going to just let him dismiss you like that?"

"Don't talk to your mother as if she was a servant."

"Me?" Craig looked uncomprehending. "You're the one who just gave her her marching orders because the master has to get back to work."

Sarah said nothing, took up the cups and left the room. Why couldn't they get along? Even for a few minutes?

"You'll have to call the police," said Craig.

"Call the police? Why?"

"About this call. If someone is going around making phone calls and pretending to be Ransom Blaisdell, the police will want to know about it. They haven't solved his murder yet. The caller might be the person who killed him. We don't know."

"I don't remember you being so eager to help the police back in your pig-baiting days."

"What? I can't believe you said that. Here we are talking about something that's happened here and now and you bring up ancient history, some kind of generation-gap argument we might have had when I was in high school. And anyway, when did I ever say the police didn't have a necessary function to perform? And when did I ever get in trouble with them? And you're the law-and-order man. How can you sit there and propose to do nothing about this?"

"I don't believe in bothering the police with something that is totally irrelevant to their investigations. This is just somebody's idea of a joke."

"But whose? And why? Why would someone's idea of a joke be to call up you of all people and claim to be Ransom Blaisdell?"

"I don't know why."

"And yet you're perfectly willing to conclude that that's what's happening. I don't understand it."

"You don't have to understand it."

"If you don't call the police, I know mom will."

"Your mother will do nothing of the kind."

"She'll do as she likes."

"Yes, she will, and I will not have you browbeating her to call the police about this. It would simply be a waste of their time."

"What if this guy calls again? Will you call the police then?"

"If I think it serves a useful purpose."

"That's for you to decide?"

"As a citizen, it is my duty to decide."

"I have never heard such a bunch of bullshit in my life."

Craig left the study. He found his mother in the kitchen, where she was washing the cups and a pan.

"Why do you have to upset him like that?" Sarah asked.

"He was already upset. By that phone call."

"I should never have told him about it."

"Why? Why should it bother him that much?"

His mother turned to face him. There was bewilderment and fear on her face. "Craig, I don't know. I don't know why."

"You should call the police and tell them."

"Why should I? What good would it do?"

"That's for them to decide."

"I won't do it against your father's wishes."

They could hear the typewriter clicking again from the study, crashing away at two hundred words per minute. Sarah smiled, as if a weight were off her shoulders.

Craig shook his head. "He's not writing. He may be typing 'the quick brown fox jumped over the lazy dog' over and over again to put up a good front, but he's not writing. You can bet that. He's scared out of his wits, mom."

Sarah didn't say anything. She put the cups away.

"Well, are you going to call them?"

"Don't talk so loud. You'll disturb your father."

"You think he can't type nonsense with voices in the background?"

"He's writing his novel. You know how single-minded he is when he gets to writing something. He's put this whole thing out of his mind."

"I'm tempted to go in there and see."

"Don't you dare," she said, spacing her words carefully. Craig was used to her protecting his father but had never seen her quite so ferocious about it. "If what you thought were true, it would be an unforgivable and useless act of malice to try to prove it."

After a pause, Craig said softly, "You're right, mom. I agree with you."

66

He saw his mother's eyes widen and her head bob up like a frightened animal's. Straining his ears, he knew what she had heard. In the next room the telephone was ringing softly.

She darted in to answer it. Craig followed her. The clacking of the typewriter keys had stopped. Could it be that Arlen Kitchener's ears were sharp enough to hear the telephone ring from his study? Or had he simply tired of his business-as-usual charade?

"Hello," she answered it, in a quavering voice.

"Good evening. Is this Mrs. Kitchener?" She sighed audibly. It was not the rasping voice.

"Yes, it is."

"This is Stu Wellman speaking. I'm with the L.A. *News-Canvas*. I edit the book review page and do the 'Book Chat' column."

"Of course, Mr. Wellman. We enjoy your work very much."

"Thank you. I wonder if I could speak to your husband."

"I'm sorry, but he's not available right now. If you'll leave your number, I'm sure he'll call you in the morning. Is there any message? May I ask what this concerns?"

The voice on the other end paused, as if Wellman were debating with himself whether to say more. "No, I'd just like to do a general article on him for the paper, that's all."

"I'm sure he'd be very pleased. And what is your number?"

Craig saw his father standing in the study doorway, looking like a man under siege. As he listened to his wife talking to the reporter, he seemed to realize that this was not another call from his tormentor. But he didn't return to the study and his typewriter. Instead he drifted out the front door. Craig speculated that his father might be about to take up smoking again.

Craig controlled the very strong impulse to go into his father's study and see if he really had been spending the last few minutes typing "the quick brown fox jumped over the lazy dog."

8. Stu hung up the phone. "He's calling me back in the morning," he said.

Across the room, Rachel was sitting on the sofa in the middle of the one presentable room in his apartment. She had complimented him on his housekeeping. Little did she realize. He never used this room when he was at home but tried to keep it in reasonably tidy shape in the case of unexpected guests. And few had been as unexpected as she was.

He hadn't expected to invite her home. (If he had, he would have gotten the bedroom tidied up, too. That is, if she hadn't been his brother's friend.) But being a book editor instead of a restaurant critic, he hadn't realized one of his favorite eating places recently had turned into a noisy country-western bar complete with mechanical bucking bronc.

So far she had told him about *The Atlantis Courier* and the Ransom Blaisdell signature. She had then prodded him to arrange an interview with Kitchener and try to feel him out, see if it was possible to get at the truth another way. The signed book somehow was not very impressive evidence, even if it was advanced on the assumption Blaisdell had signed it when he was alive.

Stu was still skeptical but hopelessly intrigued by the whole business. He hadn't required much prodding.

After the call to Kitchener, he joined her at the sofa, at a respectful distance. Their conversation returned to her "wild talent." For purposes of argument (and, paradoxically, peace), Stu was ready to accept her version of it for a while and to discuss some of the other ramifications.

"Can you do anybody's signature? I mean, anybody who ever wrote a book and is dead?"

"No, I don't think so. The pattern seems to be that the authors whose signatures I can duplicate all worked in Hollywood at one time or another, and presumably all of them visited Vermilion's, either as regulars or occasional customers."

"Any other ground rules become apparent?"

"I always use—or they always use—a fountain pen rather than a ballpoint. I have a feeling it would be impossible for me to sign one of these books with a writing instrument that wasn't in use when the author was alive. A number of these writers died before ballpoints came in, or at least before they were common. Also, the book has to be one that was published in the author's lifetime. I mean, I couldn't sign F. Scott Fitzgerald's name to a copy of *The Last Tycoon*, because it wasn't published until after he was dead."

"If you wanted to do a Shakespeare, then, it would have to be one published in his lifetime. Not much hope."

"Besides which, he never worked in Hollywood," she said with a smile.

"God knows," Stu agreed. "Have you sold any of the signed copies yet?"

"No, but I nearly did. To an Erle Stanley Gardner collector. At least that was what he said he was. He was looking at one of the other books on the table, and when I approached him, he picked up the Gardner and said he wanted to buy it. I had a feeling he was really more interested in the other book and picked up the Gardner as a form of misdirection. He's an odd character. He's been in the store before, and I got the feeling he had an interest in Arlen Kitchener. The book he slammed shut might have been this copy of *The Atlantis Courier*. I didn't see for sure. And, for some reason, I . . . Stu, that was it!"

"What do you mean?"

"One day when he was in the store, he asked about Fodor travel guides. I had some others, but he said he had a loyalty to Fodor's even if he was no relation. That's what struck me when I saw the name Fodor in those newspaper clippings. Marvin Fodor, Ransom Blaisdell's friend. I'll bet he was Marvin Fodor, and for some reason he's been haunting Vermilion's."

"I thought Robert Benchley and Craig Rice were haunting Vermilion's."

"Not the way this guy has." She grinned. "And don't press your luck on my continued good humor."

"I'll watch it. Anyway, you didn't sell this guy the Gardner."

"For some reason, I was reluctant to sell one. Maybe in the

back of my mind, I thought what you thought: that they were really forgeries and to sell them would be dishonest. But that doesn't make sense. I know they're real, and I'm sure they're meant to be sold."

"Those dead authors have a stake in keeping Vermilion's in business?"

"Who knows?"

"Do you think they spend all their time there? The ghosts, I mean?"

Rachel searched his face for evidence that he was making fun of her, but she didn't find any. Was he starting to believe in this? Anyway, it seemed to be an honest question.

"I don't know. Who knows what you can do when you're a ghost? You may have unlimited freedom of movement, or you may be stuck in one place. I think they feel at home there. I sometimes think Uncle Oscar is there too, and they all sit around and have literary discussions."

"There's never any kind of inscription or presentation, huh?"

"That's right."

"Why, do you suppose?"

"What would the inscription say? They could inscribe them to Rachel Hennings, which by 'rational' standards would be impossible, since some of them were dead before I was born. They could inscribe them to someone they knew in their lifetimes, but to do that would be to falsify history or something. I suppose that's against the rules, just like signing posthumous works."

"I suppose so." Stu was silent for a few moments. He wanted to approach her with his previous theory, but from a different angle and without offending her. "You know, Rachel, I really am sorry about the things I said last night. You do understand, don't you?"

"But you said it wasn't you talking. It was some demon who occupied your body." She said it playfully.

"Right. That's my story and I'm sticking to it. But I still have to consider other explanations for what's happening here. I have an open mind, but I also have a theory I'd like to test. And I'd like you to listen to my theory, calmly and objectively."

"It's probably impossible to be objective, but I'm pretty calm at the moment," she said. "Let's hear it."

"Back in the days when you would visit your Uncle Oscar in

that store, the visits obviously had a very strong effect on you. You really soaked up the atmosphere, soaked up the literary lore, and on a subconscious level remembered many things that up front you had forgotten. You looked at many books, looked at many authors' signatures and signed copies. Your uncle had lots of correspondence with literary figures whose books he sold, and you saw many of those letters. Your mind absorbed everything on a total recall basis.

"Now that you've come back to the store, where you had such happy times as a child, all of that data you stored up, all of those vital pictures engraved on your mind, come back closer to the surface. You subconsciously realized that you needed some special kind of help to get the business on a paying footing. You looked at the books, and your subconscious mind told you that you could produce an accurate signature of the authors, and that that would raise the value of the books and make it possible to sell them at a greater profit. You picked up the pen, and your subconscious mind did the rest. Relatively unencumbered by the inhibitions that hold us back on a conscious level, you were able to dash off those signatures, with your artist's hands and with a clear picture in your mind of what the signature should look like, as easily as the original signer could."

"That's your same old tired theory, Stu."

"That's my theory."

"So I'm a forger."

"I'm not calling you any names. Now I know you better, I'm sure you wouldn't do anything dishonest."

She laughed. "On a conscious level, I'm honest, but deep down beneath the surface, I'm a conniving criminal, huh? Can you blame me for liking my explanation better?"

"Will you try a little experiment?"

"What?"

Stu scribbled his own signature on a scrap of paper and lay it on the coffee table in front of Rachel. "Copy my signature. One try only. But promise to do the best you can."

"All right." She took up the pen, stared at the signature for a moment, and started to write. She told herself it was only fair to be as conscientious about it as she could, not throw the job in order to impress Stu that ghosts had been at work. Her pen

71

moved more slowly than it had in autographing the books. Its movement was very tentative. After a couple of minutes, they looked at the two signatures. The result was a fair approximation, but not an exact one.

"I really did the best I could, Stu. And look at that."

"It's great," said Stu. "You really have a talent for—"

"Forgery."

"Now, now, none of those loaded words. We want to stay friends. But no kidding, that's a really good copy."

"I don't think it's so good. You couldn't fool a bank teller with it. Or an autograph dealer. Even with the naked eye, you can see how jerky it is."

"Proves my point," said Stu complacently.

"Proves *your* point? Come on. You couldn't get that copy past your mother or anybody. It proves *my* point."

"Rachel, how many people could do that well without ever having tried it before? And if you can do that well with a conscious effort, just think how much better you could do unconsciously. In a state of self-hypnosis. In a sort of semi-trance where all self-consciousness and inhibition disappears, sort of like being under sodium pentothol."

"Oh, come on, Stu," she laughed.

"I'm glad you can laugh about it, anyway."

"I can laugh about it because it's such a far-out theory."

"A far-out theory!" He guffawed. "You tell me ghosts are holding your hand, and then you say *this* is a far-out theory?"

"You have to see it from my point of view," she said. "If I accept your theory, I can't sell the books as autographed copies. It would be fraud."

"I suppose it would."

"So I have to believe in ghosts," she said.

"You do?"

"Yes, it's good business."

"It's cost effective."

They both laughed as if that were the funniest punchline in the world. Stu noted the contrast to the last time they had discussed the subject, and he liked it much better this way.

In the few moments it took their mutual mirth to subside,

Rachel realized, there had been a subtle change in their positions on the sofa. First they had started leaning against each other. Then Stu had put his arm around her, and her head was resting against his shoulder, and they were sitting very close together. Stu was looking into her eyes, and his expression was changing from humor to uneasiness with a stop in between she couldn't identify or was afraid to.

"Stu," she said with enforced seriousness, "I think we'll just have to agree to disagree on this point."

"Yes, I think so," he said.

For a while, they didn't talk and didn't move. Stu was thinking that to jump away now would be to make too much of a little thing. They were getting to be friends, and friends often sat with their bodies pressed together like sardines. It didn't mean anything.

"I wonder if you shouldn't go public with this," he said after a bit.

"Go public?"

"Sure, with something like this, you could get on any talk show in the country."

"Come on, Stu."

"You could. And if your automatic autographing became famous, one of those books signed from the grave through you might become even more valuable than the real thing. No, I don't mean to say the real thing, I mean a copy signed by the author in his lifetime. You could really go places with this."

She shook her head. Her hair tickled his chin. "I'm not that type of person, Stu. I don't mean there's anything wrong with thinking in terms of publicity and a media event. For somebody in your business, it must come naturally. But I'm a quiet person. I don't need or want a lot of people around me. I couldn't handle it. And I've read about those women who were involved with automatic writing. I don't want to be subjected to the kind of probing analysis they were. I don't think my temperament is suited to being a nine-day wonder, and I'm determined to keep this whole business on as small a scale as possible. Besides, I don't know if my friends would like me to exploit them in that way."

"Fitzgerald and some of those other guys had a great publicity sense, you know."

She looked up at him. "I gave you a great item for your column, . Stu. About Arlen Kitchener and Ransom Blaisdell, I mean. What do you want from me?"

"What do I want from you?" he said softly. "A straight line, such a straight line."

He found himself kissing her. He found his tongue probing the inside of her mouth. No, honestly, he didn't find it there. He sent it there. But a few moments later, he broke off a pleasurable stroking of her thigh and drew back.

"What's the matter?" she said.

"What do you think?"

"Rod doesn't have any kind of hold over me, you know."

"He thinks he does. Or if not a hold, territorial rights."

"Territorial rights? I don't believe you said that as we sit here in the nineteen eighties."

He looked unconvinced.

"I haven't even had a letter from Rod since I've been here, Stu. Not even one letter."

"I told you, he doesn't write letters. I haven't had a letter from him in years. He uses the telephone."

"He hasn't called me."

"He's too proud. He's called me. He's very concerned about you."

"Far be it from me to cause a family quarrel. What am I, Mata Hari trying to tempt you to turn double agent? What is going on here?"

She gripped his face in two hands and willed him to resume the interrupted kiss.

And then the phone rang.

She grunted an objection, but Stu reached for it. He couldn't leave a telephone unanswered. It made a stronger call to him than anything, as he quickly demonstrated. His voice did seem a little irritated, however, when he said, "Hello."

His eyes drifted to the ceiling in the classic comic reaction.

"Hi, Rodney. How are you? . . . Well, isn't that nice. When does your flight get in? . . . Oh, she's just fine. . . . Yes, I just talked to her today. . . . I don't sound like myself? Well, ask me an intimate question about our childhood, Roddy, and I'll try to prove who I am. . . . Yes, I'll try to meet the plane. If I can't, I'll leave you a message. . . . Okay. We'll see you. . . . That's an editorial we, of course."

After he hung up, Rachel said, "Why didn't you tell him I was here? Maybe I'd have liked to talk to him."

"No, you wouldn't."

"Maybe I would."

"But you'd have liked me to say, 'She's right here, sitting across the room from me.' "

"Half naked and soon to be all."

"What kind of a woman are you, Rachel, coming between two loving brothers? A one-woman civil war."

He said it kiddingly, but she had the feeling the evening's entertainment was over.

"When is he coming in?"

"Tomorrow evening. Well, look, I'll have a big day tomorrow, what with interviewing Kitchener, if he chooses to call me back, and getting Rod at the airport and all, and you'll have a big day at the bookstore."

"Yeah," she said. "I don't want to tell Rod anything about the signing of the books and all, and I hope you won't either. Anything that smacks of spiritualism or the occult he rejects like a stone wall. I know him that well. So please don't say anything to him."

"You do want to see him though? This whole thing could be very awkward."

"Of course, I want to see him. I like Rod. And I don't intend to be awkward. Any awkwardness will be—"

"All in the family, yeah. So can I drive you back to the shop? It is getting late."

"Okay," she sighed.

The stretch of Santa Monica Boulevard that Vermilion's occupied was still very much alive at one in the morning when Stu Wellman pulled up at the curb, but the store front was dark. He walked Rachel up to the door.

She put her key in the door, rattled the knob a little, and said to Stu, a note of concern in her voice, "I think the lock's broken."

"Is it?" He tried the door, which swung open. "I'm afraid somebody's broken in."

She gasped and started through the door, but he stopped her.

"The accepted procedure for people in this situation is to call the police and not enter. Somebody might still be in there."

"Well, that's all the more reason to go in. Besides, I don't want to involve the police."

"If your store's been burgled?" Stu said.

"I'd have to see what's missing or what damage has been done first."

"Is this still your publicity phobia? Let's be sensible and call the police."

"You can call them if you want to. I'm going in the store. If there *was* anyone in there, we've given him plenty of time to get out the back way anyway."

"If you insist on going in, I'm going in first," Stu told her. He entered the store, groping for the light switch.

"The switches are at the back," Rachel whispered. "But I keep a flashlight in the desk here." She groped in a drawer and pulled the flashlight out.

"Why didn't we go in the back way?"

"Because you pulled up in front."

"You could have told me."

"I like going in this way. Usually." She flashed the light over the shelves of books. Nothing appeared to be disturbed.

"Let me have it," said Stu, and he crept down the aisle between the shelves ahead of her. She gripped his arm and followed. Suddenly she felt him tensing and he stopped abruptly.

"What's the matter?" she asked.

"There's somebody here. In one of those black leather chairs. He looks . . . he doesn't look too good."

She stood on her toes to look over his shoulder. He flashed the light on the face of the man sitting on the chair. His eyes and his mouth were open and there was a small red hole in his forehead. There was a lot of blood, running down his face and striping his beard.

"No," she said in a horrified voice. To Stu's relief, she did not scream.

"Turn around!" he said. "We both don't have to look at this."

She did. "Do you think he's . . . ?"

"I think he's dead, yes. Let me get the lights on, and you go up to the front of the store and call the police. Okay?"

"Okay."

Giving the body a wide berth, he made his way to the light switches and turned them on. The light that flooded the store now made him feel a little better, except for one factor. The light made the body in the chair look all the more obviously dead.

He heard Rachel's voice speaking into the phone in hushed tones. She was keeping her head, which gave him all the more incentive not to get sick or hysterical himself. He carried the flashlight back to the front of the store.

"They're on their way," she said. "Is the back door locked or unlocked?"

"I didn't check. I think we should stay up here, away from the body, and not tamper with anything. I doubt if anybody will be coming in the back door to carry him away."

"I just wish I could make sure nothing else is missing."

"What do you mean nothing else?"

"That copy of *The Atlantis Courier* I left on the table. It's gone, Stu."

"Are you sure?"

"Yes."

"Do you know the guy? I know you didn't get a very good look at him, and I don't want you to look again before you have to, but did you recognize him?"

"Yes, I think so. He was the man with the beard. The man who tried to buy the signed Gardner today. And I'll be surprised if his name wasn't Marvin Fodor."

9. Rachel was determined not to lie to the police. There was no point to it, no reason for it. But there was one fact she was not going to reveal unless she had to. After all, most police were still skeptical of using psychics to help in criminal investigations. Anything even farther beyond the normal than that would undoubtedly be more than they could handle and would only cause them to think she was crazy.

She would not lie, though. She would equivocate. If Stu chose to tell them, well, they'd be told, but they couldn't say she lied.

The principal police investigator was a tall moustached Chicano with matinee-idol looks that, she thought from his manner, probably embarrassed him a bit. His name was Manuel Gonzales. She somehow expected him to have a military-like rank, lieutenant or sergeant, but he said his only title was Detective, adding with a smile that the lieutenant was a guy who sat on his duff and gave orders. He and his partner, Detective Ed Jorgensen, had been on the scene in the bookstore for a couple of hours now. It was nearly dawn.

She and Stu had first been questioned by a pair of uniformed patrolmen, then the two plainclothes detectives. Meanwhile various technicians were dusting for fingerprints, photographing the body, and making a minute inspection of the crime scene. A dizzying variety of personnel had visited the scene, some of them apparently police officials of high rank. The front and back of the store were guarded by patrolmen, to keep out any nocturnal curiosity seekers, and a smaller area was roped off inside the store to keep anyone without an official function to perform away from the actual location of the body.

Now that the body was gone, Stu had (somewhat reluctantly) accepted release, and Detective Gonzales was accompanying her on a walk through the store in an effort to ascertain whether anything was missing. "I can't see two people breaking into the store so that one of them could waste the other, can you?"

"No." She smiled faintly.

"They must have been after something, and only one of them is still here. So the something is probably gone. Right?"

"If the something was ever here," she said.

"They must have thought it was."

So they walked through the store. Gonzales was very patient. She found herself dawdling in areas where the possibility of theft was small, as if trying to avoid the real truth, centered around the coffee table and the rolltop desk in the back. How could she say what was missing without telling part of the truth she was determined not to tell? There was nothing to do but plunge in.

"Yes, there is something missing. A book."

Gonzales said nothing, unwilling to provide the straight line of inquiry. He just looked at her, his brown eyes politely curious, waiting for her to tell him.

"It was a book that my Uncle Oscar had apparently acquired shortly before his death, along with a few other boxes full. I remember the book because there was something unusual about it. There was a name signed on the flyleaf. It was not the name of the author."

"Is that unusual? A former owner, no doubt."

"I don't think so."

"Do you remember the name of the book?"

"Certainly. It was *The Atlantis Courier* by Arlen Kitchener."

"Mm. Good writer. I've read some of his stuff. And what was the name that was signed on it?"

"Ransom Blaisdell," she said, looking at his eyes for a flicker of recognition. She saw nothing. Either he didn't keep up to date on unsolved murders in his city, which was extremely unlikely, or he would make a great poker player.

"I see. And why don't you think this Blaisdell was the former owner?"

"Well, Blaisdell was a writer himself. I don't think a writer would sign his name in another writer's book. They don't do that as a rule."

"How do you know Blaisdell was a writer? Did you know him?"

"No, but a book dealer gets to know a great many names in the course of business."

"You hadn't been in the business very long, had you?"

"I worked in a bookstore in Tempe, Arizona, before I came here."

"And you sold this Blaisdell's books?"

"Not that I can recall." Tiring of the apparently pointless sparring match, like a desultory tennis warmup, she laid the whole thing out for him. "Detective Gonzales, I know that Ransom Blaisdell was murdered, and I have a feeling you do, too. I also know that he was a ghostwriter. Do you know what that is?"

"Sure. He wrote books for other people."

"Yes. So as soon as I saw his name in a book signed by someone else, I considered it highly possible that he was the actual author. Now, when the book disappears and another man is murdered, I think there might be some connection. When the bearded man was in the shop earlier today, he was looking at some books on that table. He slammed another book shut and then offered to buy a book by Gardner, but I don't think that was the book he was really interested in. I think he saw the book signed by Blaisdell and wanted it, but he didn't want to let me know which one he was interested in, for fear I wouldn't sell it to him, and I'd be tipped off somehow."

"Tipped off? I don't understand."

"If I understood the significance of Blaisdell signing Arlen Kitchener's book, I might try to use it to my own advantage. I think he showed interest in the Gardner book to divert my attention, then decided to come back here at night and steal the book he really wanted."

"And he brought someone else with him."

"Or someone followed him. Or he arranged to meet someone here. I don't know. But I think that copy of *The Atlantis Courier* is the key to the whole thing. I think you should look into it."

"I think I know my job," said Gonzales mildly. "You said this guy had been in your store several times. Do you know who he was?"

"I'm not sure," she said, "but I think he could have been Marvin Fodor." She told the story of the bearded man's remark about the travel guides.

"You've been very helpful, Miss Hennings, given us a lot to work with. You must be tired. It's been a long night."

"Yes, it has."

"One more thing, and then I'll let you get some rest. Do you know where your uncle got the group of books this one was in?"

"No," said Rachel. She knew that the origin of the book was totally irrelevant, but of course Gonzales would think the book came into the store signed. What else could he think?

"It might be helpful if we could trace it to its source. See if the previous owner knew where it came from, under what circumstances Blaisdell might have signed it, and so forth."

"I can check my uncle's records and try to find out," said Rachel. She wanted to tell him to forget that part of it and just concentrate on investigating Arlen Kitchener. She didn't really want to make needless work for the police.

"I'd appreciate that. As soon as you can, but you needn't try to do it tonight." Tonight? It was nearing full daylight outside. "Get some rest. You really do look tired."

"Getting the shop ready to reopen has been tiring, but I'm really okay. In fact, I'd like to know if it's all right to open today."

"Do you really want to? I was thinking you've had a rough night. You might want to take it easy."

She did feel exhausted but anything but sleepy. "I'd just like to know when I can open again. If I want to."

"Give us till noon. I'll leave a man on duty downstairs at least until then, so you don't need to worry about being in any danger."

She laughed nervously. "It didn't even occur to me until you mentioned it."

"There's no reason to think anyone is after you, Miss Hennings. But we have to keep it in mind. It's your store."

Back in her apartment, she considered calling Stu. Would he be going to work this morning, after having been released only two hours ago? Surely he'd be asleep now. She decided to call him at the paper at nine.

It seemed to be only moments later when she realized she had gone to sleep and overshot nine o'clock by two hours.

Stu could have been reached at the offices of the *News-Canvas* long before nine o'clock. He was busy filing a story on the murder for the afternoon final. It was far from his usual beat, and he had no real reason yet for thinking he would be assigned to follow the story to its conclusion.

At the time he had left the bookstore, the police had not yet been ready to (or able to) identify the victim, except as the bearded Gardner collector of the day before.

The third of several calls to police headquarters that morning brought confirmation of the identity of the victim. As Rachel had surmised, he was Marvin Fodor, a schoolteacher in the San Fernando Valley and a friend of Ransom Blaisdell.

Going through the arts page editor, to whom he reported directly, Stu gained an interview with the managing editor.

"I want to get on this story full time, Bill. I think it's something big. It has a close connection to the book beat I normally cover, and I want an inside track on it."

"You're involved?"

"Not involved really, no."

"You helped find the body."

"Well, I like to help out when I can, yeah."

"I don't know what your relationship is with the girl in the bookstore—"

"And you're not about to, either."

"—but I think someone with a little more detachment, someone not quite so closely associated with one of the principals, would—"

"Who says she's one of the principals?"

"The body was found in her store."

"When a gangster gets blown away sitting in a barber chair, is the barber one of the principals?"

"This is an organized crime thing?"

"No, no. But it involves some big names in the best-seller business. Really big. The bookstore just happened to be where the crime took place. The girl has nothing to do with it."

The managing editor wiped his brow, an odd gesture since the office was cool and his brow wasn't wet. "I step on toes when I do this stuff. The city editor will have to agree to it, of course, and his crime reporter won't like being aced out."

Stu shrugged. "We can both work on it. It'll be big enough, believe me. Look, Arlen Kitchener may be heavily involved in this thing."

The editor looked up, interested. "Kitchener?"

"Yeah. And I called him last night requesting an interview. Just a routine interview. This morning he called back and we made an appointment for lunch today. The police may not even know yet that he has anything to do with this. It's quite likely I'll get to him before they even have the chance."

"How do you know if the police don't? No, on second thought, don't tell me. I'd rather not know." The editor drummed his fingers and tugged his ear. He collected nervous habits the way some people collected stamps. "How does Myra feel about this?" Myra was the arts editor.

"The whole idea of it drives her nuts."

The editor grinned. "Okay, get on it. I'll try to smooth everybody's feathers. You know how I want this story?"

"Sensational yet not libelous. Colorful, dramatic, and one hundred percent accurate."

"You got it. Anybody else on this? The *Times*? The TV stations?"

"No reason to think so. It's all ours."

"That's very, very good."

Shortly after getting up, Rachel tried to call Stu at the *News-Canvas*, but he'd already left, probably for his interview with Arlen Kitchener. It piqued her slightly not to be there, too, but her presence would only make it more difficult for Stu to get what information he could out of Kitchener.

So what was her fate? To sit or lie here and await word? This place could use a widow's walk.

After breakfast, she ventured down the stairs to the dark shop. A quick check of one of the all-news radio stations had indicated that the murder at Vermilion's was already being widely reported. Probably reopening the shop today would not be such a good idea, even if the police would allow it.

She wished she could do some detective work of her own. The

one way she could think of was to visit some other book dealers. Uncle Oscar had often talked of his fellow dealers. He seemed to know them all. The massive family operation in Long Beach, Acres of Books; the shop in Hollywood of years gone by, owned by the red-haired lady and her cats; the octogenarian actor whose two seemingly chaotic shops in Ocean Park surely contained a copy of every book ever written—and he had known where all of them were. Rachel sometimes wondered how used book store proprietors managed to make a living. And she knew Uncle Oscar did, too, since he really didn't have to worry about the profitability of his business.

But she knew few of the current used book dealers by name. Most of Uncle Oscar's contemporaries would be dead or out of business, and the few she knew (like that funny old science fiction specialist they called Rocket or something like that) she didn't know how to locate. She knew, though, where a good bit of the local book trade was concentrated: Hollywood Boulevard.

Maybe she could turn up another copy of *The Atlantis Courier* with which to tempt the ghost of Ransom Blaisdell. If only she could get out of here without drawing a crowd.

She didn't even turn on a light in the shop but dropped into one of the chairs around the back table. Vermilion's had now been the scene of burglary and murder, and the aura of menace couldn't be shaken completely. But somehow she felt much more comfortable here than seemed possible or logical.

Was there really anybody here? She had felt one day last week that a Fitzgerald collector had been drawn instinctively to Fitzgerald's chair. Sometimes customers would hang around and talk for no reason. The shop seemed to radiate good feeling to others just as it did to her. Used books weren't about commerce as new books were. New book stores sometimes seemed more and more depressing, following as they did the literary (or marketing) trend of the moment. Used book stores had less elbowing for position on their shelves, and maybe the books felt more comfortable just as the proprietor and the customers did. A lost classic or a forgotten idea or a failed vogue could wait here on the shelves for years and years, waiting for its reader. The smell

84

of dust was a small price to pay for the miracle of a used bookstore.

But friendly and therapeutic as it was, Vermilion's would not welcome its customers today. They would have to jostle for position among the shelves with the police and press. Rachel sighed and returned upstairs.

Stu arrived for his lunchtime meeting with Arlen Kitchener a few minutes early. The place they'd agreed to meet was a rather dark and probably overpriced French restaurant on La Cienega. Stu had never been there before, but Kitchener had insisted it was a good place. Stu concluded Kitchener expected to pick up the check. It was all the same to Stu, because he would claim the expenses from the paper if he wound up paying.

As the maitre d' guided him through the labyrinth to Kitchener's table, Stu noticed the author was already in close conversation with another man whom Stu didn't recognize. He hoped it wasn't a plainclothes detective. Certainly Kitchener looked worried enough.

The two men rose as Stu approached. Kitchener was somewhat shorter than he remembered, but he was certainly an imposing figure, only the thick head of all-white hair betraying his age. The other man was overweight and comparatively colorless in rather a baggy gray suit. His most distinguishing characteristic was an obvious toupee.

"Mr. Wellman, you're early," said Kitchener. "Fortunately, I'm even earlier."

"I'd say something about birds and worms, but you might take it wrong," said Stu.

The novelist laughed insincerely. "Clarence, do you know Stu Wellman of the *Herald-Examiner?*"

"*News-Canvas,*" Stu corrected him.

"Of course. Mr. Wellman, this is my agent, Clarence Gustavson."

They shook hands. Gustavson said, "The agent meets the journalist. One necessary evil greets another, eh, Arlen?"

Arlen half laughed as if he weren't sure whether that had been a joke or a proverb poorly translated from the Danish. The good humor of both men seemed forced to Stu. Something was bothering these two.

"Well," said Gustavson, "I'll run along now. Unless you think you should be represented by counsel, Arlen."

Kitchener gave him a sharp look. The agent didn't miss it and appeared somewhat taken aback.

"I don't think the interview is going to be quite that much of an ordeal," said Stu.

"I hope not," said Clarence Gustavson. "I was joking of course."

"Yes, well, thank you, Clarence," said Kitchener. "We'll stay in touch."

"We always do," said Gustavson, who nodded to Stu and crept off.

The two men sat down. Stu realized that the novelist was extremely jumpy. Stu, who recognized the agent's flippant conversational style as something very akin to his own, had found the offhand remark harmless, if not notably funny, but it seemed to have hit Arlen Kitchener where he lived.

Kitchener had a drink in front of him, and now he downed it in one gulp. Then he asked Stu what he was drinking and beckoned the cocktail waitress over.

Stu asked for a beer. He had the feeling Kitchener was looking at him as though he had made a social gaffe, but it didn't bother him. By the time the waitress had left, Kitchener seemed to be his smooth self again.

"He's a very good man," said Kitchener.

"Who? Gustavson?"

"A very fine agent, totally loyal, totally honest. And that's very important, very precious. Impossible to overestimate."

"Even if his jokes make you nervous?"

He wasn't sure how Kitchener would react to that sally. He was disappointed. The author smiled expansively.

"Mr. Wellman, many of my acquaintances believe me to be an almost totally humorless man. I don't think that is really a fair charge, but it often seems to me that what other people find amusing just doesn't strike me that way. I sometimes wonder if it's a form of learning disability. I think I understand people well enough, and I have written several novels that I believe would attest to that fact, but humor is not one of my strong suits. I don't think I'm humorless, but perhaps my sense of humor is different from other people's."

The cocktail waitress delivered Stu's beer, and Stu nodded and lofted his glass in a toasting gesture.

"We can test that," he said. "Tell me your favorite joke."

Kitchener seemed to think seriously about the request. Finally, he said, "I can't think of one. I don't seem to think in terms of jokes. Well, Mr. Wellman, I am totally at your disposal. What would you like to know?"

All during the sparring, Stu had been thinking of various ways to approach this interview, but even now he wasn't sure just where he was going with it or what he expected to get out of Kitchener. The novelist, whether he knew any jokes or not, was a practiced interviewee and was not likely to be thrown easily. Now he seemed very cool, having overcome whatever it was his agent had said to throw him off. Probably he already knew about the murder and its possible significance. In fact, it was hardly impossible that he knew about both murders before anyone else did. If covering up the ghosting job on *The Atlantis Courier* was important enough to him, he might even have killed Fodor to do it. Presumably, Fodor had seen the signed book while he had been in the store yesterday, and there was no reason to be certain that Rachel or anyone else had looked at the book and remembered it, or made any theories about its significance.

"Well, Mr. Wellman?" Arlen was too polite to say out loud, "I'm a busy man," but that was what his eyes seemed to be saying.

Stu decided to start with something inconsequential. "How do you write, Mr. Kitchener? By hand? Manual typewriter? Electric? Word processor?"

"IBM Selectric. That is as advanced a model as I choose to get into. I've thought about word processors, but I fear the change would be too radical for me. I enjoy putting paper in the machine, and I would miss the noise of the keys striking."

Stu nodded. "I know what you mean. We have word processors in the office, but some guys insist on using old manuals they've had with them since they started in the newspaper business.

There was an old guy who retired last year still using a machine he'd had on Guam during World War II."

"Indeed. That is carrying resistance to change rather farther than I do, but I can understand it."

"Let me ask you a rather trite question, Mr. Kitchener, but one I always like to ask writers who have written a good many books. I'd like to know what is your own favorite of the books you've written. Which one pleased you the most?"

"I'm tempted to say that my favorite is the next one, but I guess that's a trite answer as well as being a cop-out."

"I agree with your analysis entirely," Stu said.

"Yes, I thought you would. Well, of course, I have a soft spot for my first book, *Added Starter*, which was published in 1949. How the years do go by. If I tried to read it now, which I don't ever do with my old books, I'm sure I'd find it embarrassing. My first real best-seller, of course, was *Loves of a Prince*, which I like to think had something to do with the vogue for biographical fiction that has been pretty strong ever since. I could say that book changed my life, since it led to my moving out here, a move I've never regretted. And I think Edward VII was a truly fascinating figure, don't you?"

"I've tried to pattern my life after him," said Stu lightly.

Arlen took the remark seriously. "It's not impossible. Yes, that was a good book, but I had the facts of history to guide me, so it was not an entirely creative work on my part. *The Hungerford Inquiry* was a good one. I think on balance, though, I'd have to say my best was *Cock, Still Your Crowing*, even though I wrote it twenty years ago. Have you read it?"

An awkward question. Stu had read two or three of Kitchener's novels, finding them for the most part flabby, overwritten, and obvious, among other less complimentary adjectives. *Cock, Still Your Crowing* was not one of them.

"I think I missed that one. Wanted to read it, of course, but in my business, if you don't get a review copy, and if you don't read something just when it comes out, you never quite get around to it. I'll read it now, though. Now my own favorite of the books of yours I have read was *The Atlantis Courier*. I thought that was a really fine book." The statement was almost truthful.

"My son agrees with you. I can't say I do. I thought that book was entirely too preachy and didactic. And far, far from my best work."

"Did you think so while you were writing it, or on rereading it later?"

"Neither. I don't often reread my own work, as I've said. But on reflection that was what I thought of it. I thought it was a lousy book, if you want to know the truth." Kitchener said it almost fiercely.

"How did you happen to write a book so different from your others?"

Kitchener seemed to backpedal now. "Well, I don't think it was so different really, in intent or in execution. I always try to balance entertainment with information in my novels, and the material in that book about the environment and so forth was based on really genuine concerns that I have about—uh—things like that. It was just that the message I was trying to put across overbalanced the story, and I think I am basically a storyteller. Now, in *Cock, Still Your Crowing,* the balance was perfect in my opinion. You could learn just about everything you would want or need to know about the poultry industry in that novel, but that wasn't what kept people reading at all. It was the love story and the conflict of the old man with his son, and the difficulty he had in accepting new methods in the business. And of course, the labor strife contributed to the suspense as well, though I tried not to get too political with it. By the way, Wellman, you don't look more than in your mid-thirties at the most, am I right?"

"Uh, yes."

"Then how could you have expected to get a review copy of a book written twenty years ago? You must have been a very young book editor at that time."

"Ah, wasn't there a reprint?"

"Well, it's been continuously in print in paperback. I'll send you a copy. You really should read it, whether you were sincere in saying you wanted to or not."

"I was completely sincere. How do you go about doing your research for one of these big novels?"

"Well, on *Swift and Speedy Trial,* I spent five hundred hours in

89

courtrooms. On *Cock, Still Your Crowing,* I must have spent a like number of hours—"

"In chicken coops?"

"Not precisely in the coops, no. Was that supposed to be funny?"

"Not really. Just a reflex, like when the doctor taps you on the knee."

"Now *The Hungerford Inquiry* had a medical background, so I—"

"I was thinking about *The Atlantis Courier.*"

"Why are you so interested in that particular book? Actually, my research was rushed on that one, not nearly the amount of time I normally put in."

"Even though it was so deeply felt and sincere in its message that your desire to educate got away from you?"

The waiter arrived to take their order at what Stu thought was a very inopportune time. He had the feeling he was on the edge of finding something out, but the interruption gave Kitchener a chance to hesitate over his menu for a moment and mentally regroup. Still, if the interview got too hostile, Kitchener could just tell him to get lost. He probably wouldn't, though, because that in itself was an admission.

Kitchener ordered the dover sole, Stu a steak sandwich.

When the waiter had left, Kitchener said, "You know, young man, I spent enough time in courtrooms researching *Swift and Speedy Trial* to recognize a cross-examination technique when I hear one. I realize you're just out to get a good interview, but I wonder if you didn't miss your calling."

Stu smiled. "Why would I be cross-examining you? That doesn't sound very friendly."

"That's one of the problems with it, yes."

"I've been trying to remember where I know your agent from."

"Clarence? I thought a book editor would know all the major agents?"

"I know publishing company publicists and editors and press agents, but not many literary agents, I'm afraid. Most of them are headquartered in New York."

"Well, Clarence came out here at the same time I did."

"Are you his only client?"

"Oh, no, he has other clients. But not many."

"With the money you make him, he probably doesn't need many."

"I don't know about that. He has an office and a secretary, and I have no idea what his expenses are. I hope you don't want to talk about financial matters."

"No, no, just literary." Stu feigned a sudden inspiration. "I know where I remember him from. Or his name anyway. Didn't he represent Ransom Blaisdell?"

It was a stunt, and Stu decided immediately it was a successful one. Kitchener tried with some success not to let anything show on his face, but from across the table, Stu could almost feel his body tensing up.

"Who?"

"Ransom Blaisdell, the writer who was murdered a couple of months ago."

"Oh, yes, I remember, of course. I didn't know the man. Never met him. But I believe I do remember reading that Clarence was his agent."

"Didn't you ever discuss him?"

"No. Are you surprised? Why should I discuss my agent's other clients with him?"

"Well, I thought that after the murder and everything, when one of his other clients had been murdered . . . I mean, you and Mr. Gustavson are close friends, aren't you? You came out here together and all."

"Mr. Wellman, just what are you getting at? Just what is it you want to know? This is not at all the sort of interview you led me to expect."

Stu did his best to look innocent. "Really? I'm sorry. I didn't know when I talked to you about the murder at Vermilion's bookstore, and I suppose you didn't either. Of course, the crime beat has nothing to do with me, but I can understand why you would be a bit nervous, under the circumstances, especially in view of that book that was stolen."

Kitchener lay his hand flat on the restaurant table and leaned across the table at Stu. "Mr. Wellman, I don't know what the hell you're talking about."

"Oh, well, I guess I've missed the boat again. I couldn't help noticing that you and Gustavson were a little, well, agitated in your conversation when I came up, and naturally I assumed you were talking about the murder, maybe one of you was telling the other about it or something. But that has nothing to do with our interview, and I'm sorry I brought it up. I wanted to ask you about *Loves of a Prince*. Did the royal family give you any cooperation when you were working on that? Were they surprised that an American writer would . . . ?"

Arlen Kitchener was staring hard at Stu. "Wellman, I don't know what kind of a game it is—"

He broke off as the waiter brought their orders. Stu poked his steak to make sure it was medium, as he'd ordered it. When the waiter left, it was as though the bell had rung for the next round. Showing no interest in his fish but seemingly controlling the anger that had seemed ready to erupt, Kitchener merely said, "Mr. Wellman, I do not know about this recent murder you are referring to, or what it has to do with me. Maybe you could enlighten me. Was it anyone I know? I'm sure you'll understand my reluctance to continue the interview until you clear this up for me."

Stu unconcernedly put a piece of steak in his mouth. "I don't know if you know him or not. A fellow named Marvin Fodor. He was found dead in Vermilion's bookstore early this morning. I understand he was a friend of Ransom Blaisdell's."

"I still don't see how I fit into this."

"Blaisdell means nothing to you, huh? That's why you almost had a stroke when I mentioned his name."

"What are you getting at, Wellman?"

"Were any of your other books ghostwritten, or was it just the one?"

"None of my books were ever ghostwritten."

"There are rumors."

"I don't know about any rumors. But if your paper prints anything to that effect, you can expect a lawsuit, I promise you."

"Why would Ransom Blaisdell sign a copy of your book, then?"

"How should I know? He may have owned a copy and written his name in it."

"Would you do that?"

"Would I? I have bookplates."

"Bookplates, sure. But would you, a novelist, write your name in John Hancock–size script across the flyleaf of another writer's book?"

"Of course not. But I have no idea what a person like Ransom Blaisdell might do."

"A person like Ransom Blaisdell? I thought you didn't know him."

"I didn't."

"Then how do you know what kind of a person he was?"

"I read about him in the paper. Anyway, I didn't say I knew anything about him. Mr. Wellman, I give you my word of honor as a gentleman. I never in my life met Ransom Blaisdell. Never."

Stu found he was honestly enjoying his steak. It must, he reflected, be a deep-seated sadistic streak. Watching Kitchener squirm gave him an appetite. As for the sole cooling off on the novelist's plate, it might as well still be swimming.

"Ghostwriting is quite an interesting topic, Mr. Kitchener. The *Times* did a whole spread on it a couple of years ago. Did you ever do any ghostwriting yourself?"

"No, never, unless you count some speeches for a politician, which is not quite the same thing. Every word of fiction I ever wrote, I am proud to say, appeared under my own name. And furthermore, I wrote every word of *The Atlantis Courier* myself."

Stu almost dropped his fork. It was too good to be true. *"The Atlantis Courier?* Is that what you said?"

"Yes, you accused me—"

"I never mentioned any title, Mr. Kitchener."

"You've been talking about that damn book ever since we sat down here."

"Maybe so, but I never said that was the book I thought had been ghosted. You brought that up. I was asking you a question about *Loves of a Prince.*"

"You were talking about *The Atlantis Courier.* You kept dwelling on it."

"Mr. Kitchener, a copy of *Atlantis Courier,* signed by Ransom Blaisdell, disappeared from Vermilion's last night at the time of the murder of this Mr. Fodor. A natural hypothesis is that the

93

book suggested Blaisdell was the true author, and that it was taken to keep that information from becoming known. I would appreciate a statement from you about this for my story."

"Which is strictly literary?" Kitchener apparently was capable of sarcasm if not humor.

"It is a literary question, Mr. Kitchener. Did you write *The Atlantis Courier*? Or did Ransom Blaisdell?"

Arlen Kitchener stood up from the table. "Mr. Wellman, I have no intention of dignifying that question by answering it. And let me reiterate what I said would happen if your paper persists in spreading that rumor. Good afternoon."

And he was gone. Stu would be stuck with the check after all. Not that it hadn't been worth it. On his way out of the restaurant, he stopped at a phone booth and called Vermilion's.

"He as much as admitted it, Rachel!" Stu crowed into the phone. "But I'll swear he didn't know about the murder. Or if he did, he's a hell of an actor. And if he *didn't* know about the murder, what the hell were he and Gustavson talking about when I got there? Well, that's my report. How are you doing?"

"I'm okay. Turning a little stir crazy here, though. What are you going to do next? See the agent?"

"That's a good idea. Glad I thought of it."

"I may do a little sleuthing, too."

"There at the store?"

"I don't know."

"Look, you be careful. There's a murderer running around loose."

"Scores of them on any given day in Los Angeles. You sound like somebody in Uncle Oscar's mystery section."

"Stay there in the store, where you're safe."

"That guy we found dead wasn't safe."

"But you've got cops all around you. Stay there and sign some books or something."

"While the menfolk do the hunting?"

Stu sighed. "I'll be in touch later. Don't do anything silly."

"Okay. I was planning to stand in front of the mirror doing my Bette Davis imitations, but I'll try to do something more productive." She hung up the phone laughing. Stu's conversational style was rubbing off on her.

10. Arlen Kitchener's fingers trembled as he dialed his agent's number. He felt at the end of his rope. As he'd entered the house, he'd snapped at Sarah and immediately regretted it. There had been no time to mend his fences, however. He had to lock himself in the study, make the call in private. She didn't know. No one knew.

He got the secretary. As always, when he got through, he was put on to Gustavson right away. They knew well enough which client was paying the rent on that office.

"Yes, Arlen, what is it? Not another anonymous call?"

"No. Worse than that, Clarence. Another murder."

"Another murder?"

"That damned yellow journalist from the *News-Canvas* told me about it. I'll have the police here any minute, Clarence, and they'll be asking me who wrote *The Atlantis Courier.*"

"Why? I don't understand."

Arlene gave him a quick and somewhat garbled version of what Stu Wellman had told him.

"Ransom would never have signed a copy of that book, Arlen. He was more discreet than that."

"That was certainly what you assured me, Clarence. And I surely wanted to believe you. But it seems that he wasn't as reliable as you thought. But I'm not calling to berate you. I just want to know what to do. Wellman will print it. He's convinced I told him Blaisdell ghosted it."

"Did you?"

"No, no, but he did some kind of Sherlock Holmes trick to make himself believe I made a slip. He's going to print it, Clarence, I know he is. Of course, I made a lot of noise about suing him and his paper if it ever got in print. But I'd have to back down if it happened."

"They couldn't prove Ransom did it, could they? But maybe they could, if he told someone." There was a pause. Clarence was apparently thinking. Arlen hoped to God he was thinking.

Finally, the agent said, "I don't think we could afford a court fight on it, Arlen."

"I have plenty of money, Clarence. But I wonder if—"

"I wonder, too. It might hurt us more than it would help us. I think the only course we have now is to come clean."

"Come clean?"

"Sure, admit that Blaisdell wrote *The Atlantis Courier*. Arlen, it's no crime to have somebody ghost a book for you. And if we don't admit to it, just let it lie around in the form of innuendo, there are bound to be rumors about your other books. I think a full and frank accounting is the only way to save the situation."

"But they may think I killed this man last night. Or both of them, Blaisdell too."

"Did you?"

"Of course I didn't. What do you take me for?"

"Ten percent."

"What?"

"Never mind. Look, Arlen, I know you didn't kill them. And if you admit to the ghosting now, show that it's really no big thing to you, then why would anyone figure you had a motive for killing them?"

"But the book that disappeared, Clarence."

"I don't know about that, but I'm convinced truth is our best policy here. It's the one I intend to follow."

"What? Clarence, what the hell are you saying? You have to show me some loyalty on this thing."

"Arlen, what have I been doing? When the police were questioning me about Blaisdell's death, I was very careful not to bring your name into it, not give them any reason to think you'd ever heard of Ransom Blaisdell. That was tough, but I did it. And I never had to lie to them outright. But now, they're going to come to me and ask me point blank whether a book by you, my client, was ghostwritten by Blaisdell, another client. What can I do? Can I say I don't know? I'd have to know. Do I lie and tell them it never happened? Then if their investigation turns up anything to support the allegation, I really am in trouble. I've been lying to them, obstructing their investigation. Maybe it would make me an accessory or something."

"Accessory to what? I haven't done anything!"

"Arlen, you've heard my advice, and I've told you what I'm going to do."

"But I don't want this known, Clarence. Not even Sarah knows. And that goddam crappy potboiler was the only thing ever published over my name that my son thought was any good. I'll be in disgrace before my own family, Clarence. You can't do this to me."

"I'm not doing anything to you, Arlen. In this whole business, I've done my best to save your bacon—first by finding you a ghost, then by covering up for you when he was murdered."

"You did not cover up for me."

"Arlen, we're old friends, but this is as far as we can go. I'm going to tell the truth about this. To the police when they ask me, and to Wellman when he asks me. It's the only right thing to do, and ultimately it's in my own self-interest. I have to think of myself sometimes, you know."

"When your whole career is based on me, on my work? And what's this thing about telling Wellman? What makes you think he'll ask you? Surely you're not going to go running to the newspapers to betray me."

"I don't have to run, Arlen. He's in my outer office right now. If I thought it would do any good, I'd refuse to see him or try to deflect his questions, but at this point I know the whole thing has to come out. We might as well put as good a face on it as we can."

Arlen hung up the phone. It almost slid from his hand and clattered on the table, but he grasped it at the last moment.

Someone was tapping lightly on the study door.

He went and unlocked it. It was Sarah. Her face was ravaged.

"Yes? What is it?" he said.

"The police are here to see you, Arlen. They haven't said why. Did Craig tell them about the anonymous call, do you suppose? I hoped he wouldn't."

"No, dear, I think it's about another matter. Please show them in."

His languid manner frightened her. She thought she had never seen her husband looking quite so defeated.

"I'm surprised you haven't been around to see me already, Mr. Wellman," Clarence Gustavson was saying. "I'm sure that Arlen Kitchener has nothing to do with this, but the presence of that book makes it inevitable that he, and I, would be questioned."

"Your client as good as told me that Ransom Blaisdell wrote *The Atlantis Courier,* Mr. Gustavson."

"If that is what he chose to tell you, there's not much use my denying it. It's not the sort of thing I am anxious to see in print, and neither will Arlen be. But I think we'll survive it."

"You think the public aren't interested in the fact that one of their famous best-selling novelists employs ghostwriters?"

"Two points," said Gustavson, holding up two fingers. "The plural is uncalled for. Ransom Blaisdell is the only ghostwriter who has ever written anything signed with the name Arlen Kitchener, and he worked on only the one novel. And quite a lot that you find in that novel is Arlen's. He edited the manuscript himself before submission and in fact rewrote certain passages to give them his own special touch. I don't think it's wrong to call that book a Kitchener novel. In fairness, I also don't think it was wrong for Ransom to feel he was the real author, though his agreement with us about it swore him to secrecy.

"Second point," said the agent, dropping one finger. "Sure, the public will be interested. The public is always interested in scandal, secrets, innuendos. But how much of an effect will it have on their book-buying habits. They are interested in the content of a Kitchener novel, not with who wrote this passage and who wrote that."

"Have you told the police about all this?"

"Not yet. I only found out about the crime a few minutes ago. And I'm perfectly willing to let them come to me about it." He stopped and smiled. "As long as they come to me before your article hits the streets. I don't want them to think I'm telling the press things before I tell them."

"Though you are."

"Not really. I didn't tell you Blaisdell wrote *The Atlantis Courier.* You claimed already to have that information when you came here."

"Maybe you can tell me something. Who else knew about the ghosting job?"

"The only people I discussed it with were the two writers concerned, Arlen and Ransom. I'm relatively sure that Arlen didn't tell anyone."

"Not even his family?"

"I don't think so, but please don't attribute that to me, okay?"

"Okay."

"As for Blaisdell, he *shouldn't* have told anyone. But obviously someone found out: this Fodor fellow who was killed."

"Do you have any theory on the murder, Mr. Gustavson, any idea who might have killed Fodor or why?"

"Not at all. I know very little about the thing. I can understand why someone might conclude this supposedly missing book has something to do with it, but it may very well be unconnected. I shouldn't really say anything about it until I know all the facts. The account I received was rather garbled."

"Who told you about the crime?"

"Do you reveal your sources, Mr. Wellman?"

"Sometimes, but that's another story. Did Blaisdell do any other ghosting?"

"You know he did. He wrote Candy Helms' autobiography and—"

"I know that, Mr. Gustavson. I mean did he do any other ghosting for other *writers,* not sports or entertainment personalities?"

"Certainly he did. But I'm sure you don't expect me to tell you their names. Things like that are supposed to be kept strictly secret. To reveal any of them to you would compromise me professionally, to put it mildly. Besides, it's not relevant."

"You won't tell the police either?"

"Not if it has nothing to do with this case, I won't."

"You're to decide that?"

"Of course, I am. Let me put it to you this way. If your editor was murdered tomorrow, would you immediately volunteer to the police that he once took you to a whorehouse for your birthday?"

"How did you know about that?"

Gustavson laughed. "No, really. You'd tell if you thought the madam killed him."

"My editor is a woman."

"Then the madam killed her in retaliation for leaving the racket? Or more likely she killed the madam, who had been blackmailing her? Do you like mystery stories, Mr. Wellman?"

"Some of them."

"I've always wanted a good mystery writer to represent."

"Some of Kitchener's stuff is pretty mysterious."

"Mysterious how it got published, you mean?"

"May I quote you on that?"

"I don't think so, no." The agent was really enjoying himself now. Stu wasn't. The repartee was getting him nowhere.

"Can't you give me a few leads, Mr. Gustavson? Just tell me a few names, not for attribution, of writers that Blaisdell ghosted for."

"No, I mustn't do that. I'm sorry. They'd know, you see."

"I guess so. What if I tried some names on you and you just nodded your head?"

"Or maybe we could play twenty questions. No, I'm sorry. Mr. Wellman, I know nothing about the crime. I am willing to confirm that Blaisdell wrote most of *The Atlantis Courier*. It's entertaining talking to you—I think we're kindred spirits—but I don't think there's really any more I can tell you."

"Did you know Fodor at all?"

"Not that I remember. I may have met him."

"Was Ransom Blaisdell happily married?"

"Why, I think so."

"Have you seen Mrs. Blaisdell since the death of her husband?"

"Well, yes, briefly, a few times. I was his agent, and there were matters to be cleared up."

"Was there a man in evidence? Was she shacked up with anybody?"

Gustavson smiled. "I'm afraid she didn't tell me. You don't suppose this Fodor fellow . . . ?"

"Did Mrs. Blaisdell know her husband wrote *The Atlantis Courier*?"

"Not that I know of."

"Did the question ever come up after Blaisdell's death?"

"Why should it?"

"Didn't he get any royalties from the book?"

"No, ghosting doesn't work like that, Mr. Wellman. We made a flat financial deal for delivery of the manuscript at the time

Blaisdell wrote it. He was paid for a job of work. There were no further payments after that."

"No matter how much money the book made, how many copies it sold, how much money the movies paid for it?"

"That's right. As a literary editor of a newspaper, I'd have thought you knew that much." He snorted with laughter. "But of course you do, don't you? I forgot that acting dumb is one way of getting a story."

"You're so flattering," Stu said. "Thanks for the chance to cover up my ignorance."

"Don't mention it. I'll cover yours if you'll promise not to cover mine."

Getting to his feet, Stu reached a hand across the desk. Gustavson took it. "Thanks. You've been very helpful."

"My pleasure. I'm counting on you not to make this article a hatchet job on Arlen Kitchener."

"I don't do hatchet jobs."

"Do you do windows?"

"A window on the world of books."

"I like you, Wellman. We think alike."

As Stu was leaving, he thought about that tribute and decided he didn't like it at all.

Arriving at Vermilion's Bookshop, Stu saw a film crew for Channel 4 shooting out in front. He realized how wrong he had been about the rest of the news media not being in on the story. He wondered if Rachel had talked to them and, whether she had or not, how she was handling this invasion. He parked his car around the corner and walked to the back entrance of the store. There he ran into a film crew from Channel 2. They had the poor girl surrounded.

He tapped on the back door. One of the TV film crew told him, "It's no use. There's nobody there."

"Oh?"

"Either that or she won't admit she's there. She's hiding out."

"Have you tried tear gas yet?"

The TV field reporter, a nervous little man who used too much hair spray, walked up to Stu and said, "Ahhh . . ."

"Either you think I'm a doctor and you have a sore throat, or you think I might have something to tell you and you don't know who I am."

The field reporter, who would never make anchorman, gave him an embarrassed grin. "Yeah, but I don't think you're a doctor. Who are you?"

"If I get around to the front of the store, a beautiful blonde will interview me, and she probably *would* recognize me."

The field reporter looked terrified. "You're not Arlen Kitchener, are you? I thought you were older."

"If I were Arlen Kitchener, would I be here? I'm a friend of Ms. Hennings. My name is Stu Wellman. I'm with the *News-Canvas*."

"Will you give us an interview on camera?" the little guy said hopefully.

"About the same time I give an exclusive interview to the *Times*."

"TV is tough," said the field man forlornly.

"Journalism is tough. Life is tough. I know they clean house a lot at Channel 2, but you're probably safe. You look taller in person, you know that?"

Stu strolled off. He walked around the end of the block and approached the store from the front. Channel 4 was having more luck. Why had the Channel 2 lot thought it would be so clever to attack from the rear anyway? The back of the store didn't even make a pretty picture.

The blonde was interviewing Detective Gonzales, who looked like he would have been happier in Hollywood of the twenties, when he could have gotten work as a Valentino substitute. The blonde was surprisingly chunky. Now he knew why they only photographed her from the clavicle up.

He noticed there was a CLOSED sign in the door of the store. If Rachel was in there, he'd never get to her. He drifted off and decided to try her from a phone booth a few blocks away.

He got a busy signal. Either she was talking to somebody, or she'd taken it off the hook. If only I had a helicoptor, he reflected.

He called the paper, too, and was told the crime reporter was pursuing the police angle of the thing. He had learned nothing new, however. Stu was advised to keep hitting the literary part of the story. There were two in-person calls he could make in the San Fernando Valley: Mrs. Blaisdell and Candy Helms, one of the ghostees. He decided to brave the smog and sticky heat and drive over the pass to try to talk to at least one of them. He really wanted to see Rachel, but he couldn't get to her if she was hiding under the bed.

11.

Rachel hadn't been hiding under the bed, at least not literally. She watched the scene below as much as she could from the upstairs window. She saw Detective Gonzales talking to the Channel 4 reporter. Taking the phone off the hook probably hadn't been too hot an idea either. Stu or the police might have been trying to reach her, and she was anxious to know what Stu had discovered since his lunch with Kitchener. But the calls from the press had become more and more frequent shortly after she'd last talked to Stu, and she was tired of having no comment. She was almost desperate enough to actually try some Bette Davis imitations.

Now she supposed she had better go downstairs and let Gonzales in. The lock on the door had been repaired, and as far as she knew there was no longer a police officer on duty.

She opened the door a crack for Gonzales, staying behind it in order to stay off the six o'clock news. The policeman ducked in the doorway and turned to smile at her.

"You can't stay a hermit forever, you know," he said.

"I don't like publicity," she said. "And that's putting it mildly."

"I can tell. But I don't think it's healthy locking yourself up like this."

"I feel safe here," she said.

"Eventually you'll have to eat or—"

"Fortunately, I have a full refrigerator. Have you talked to Arlen Kitchener yet?"

"Yes. He says the whole thing is nonsense, that he never used a ghostwriter in his life and we'd better see that any rumors stay out of the papers. He has friends in high places in the Police Department or City Hall or something."

"Do you believe him?"

"That he has friends?"

"No, that he didn't use a ghostwriter. I am positive that he did."

"We only have your word for it."

"Stu Wellman saw the book, too."

"Did you find out the source of that particular book?"

104

"No, my uncle's records aren't specific enough. I'm sorry. Someone could have come in off the street and sold it to him or anything. Would it help if you had another copy of the book signed by Blaisdell?"

Gonzales was surprised. "There's another one?"

"I don't know. There might be."

"And you could get a hold of it?"

"Maybe."

"How, when you don't know where the first one came from?"

"That's a good question," she smiled. "But I might be able to."

"How did you happen even to remember that book, Miss Hennings? You have a lot of books downstairs."

"When you work with books all the time, you remember things like that. Detective Gonzales, it is all right if I leave here, isn't it?"

"Of course it is. I think you should. As I say—"

"Yes, well, I think I'll have to."

"Do you have a car? I didn't see one."

"No. I guess I should get one, huh? I had a renter when I first came."

"How have you been getting around?"

"I haven't had to very much. I've ridden the buses a few times."

Gonzales shook his head. "If you expect to function in L.A., you have to have a car. The public transportation. . . . Well, you've found out about that. Look, where do you want to go? Can I take you anywhere?"

"Would you? I want to go to Hollywood Boulevard."

Gonzales made a face. "I can think of nicer places than that. It's gotten real tacky. The stars in the sidewalk are interesting, I guess, and the Chinese—"

"I'm not thinking as a tourist. I want to go there because that's the local center of my particular line of work. That's where the book dealers are."

"And you want to look for a book that will help us? Another copy of *The Atlantis Courier*?"

"Yes."

"Another copy signed by the ghostwriter is just going to jump into your hand?"

"You offered to give me a ride, Detective Gonzales. I will be able to get a bus back, won't I? I'm sure there's a Hollywood bus that goes by."

"I can pick you up when you're done. Just tell me what time. Then maybe we can have some dinner."

"You must have some more questions you want to ask me."

"Maybe. But not necessarily about the case. Mostly I just want to have dinner with you."

She considered the suggestion. "All right."

The Valley was sticky and smoggy, and Blaisdell's widow wasn't at home.

To avoid another fruitless drive, Stu telephoned the tennis player, Candy Helms, telling her he was doing an article on athletic memoirs and asking if he could come by to see her. She sounded delighted, he thought, told him to come right over. Her address was in an affluent part of Sherman Oaks.

Stu rang the doorbell and mopped his brow. It must be one of the hottest days of the summer.

The figure that answered the door set him to thinking.

It was perfectly possible that on a day as hot as today promised to be in the relaxed atmosphere of Southern California, a beautiful woman might answer the door wearing an extremely brief bikini. Maybe even if she was expecting someone, a reporter whom she had never met before. And certainly Candy Helms had no reason to want to conceal her body. No part of her looked forty.

But under the circumstances, Stu really felt she must be up to something. Fleetingly, he hoped he was up to something, too.

"Ms. Helms?"

"Yes, but call me Candy," she said. "Stu Wellman, I presume."

"That's right. It was good of you to see me. And it's good to see you."

She raised an eyebrow, and her eyes laughed at him. "Please come back to the pool," she said.

He followed her through the house, decorated with photos and trophies and various sculptures and figurines of cats, and out of the sliding glass door to the pool. Her shifting, rolling bottom was hypnotic. The danger now was not to think but to stop thinking.

"Coffee?" she offered. "Or something cold? A beer?"

"Coffee would be fine, thanks."

It must take work to keep that brown body in shape. Stu knew there were movie actresses who looked that good at forty, but really Candy Helms was out of the public eye now, wasn't even playing competitive tennis anymore. Must have great respect for the private eye.

"What do you do for exercise, Candy?" he asked.

She rolled her eyes at him in mock shock. Oddly enough, he hadn't meant it as a provocative remark. He got into enough trouble with intentional double entendres without being accused of ones that weren't really there.

"No, really," he said. "I like to know what people do to keep in shape."

"I swim, jog a bit, still play tennis quite often. What do you do for exercise?"

"Oh, I type a lot. I have very nimble fingers. And I lift boxes of books."

"Be sure to bend your knees when you do that."

"And when I get in a tough spot over something I'm writing, I get up and pace around the desk."

"Are you a sportswriter, Stu?" He had only identified himself by name in making the appointment, and she apparently was not familiar with his work. He wasn't surprised.

"Oh, no, I'm the book editor. I wanted to talk to you about your writing."

She laughed. "My writing? That'll be a short interview." The coffee was ready, and she poured them each a cup. "Cream? Sugar?"

"No, thanks, I take it black."

They carried their coffee to two long lounges by the pool. "I'm sorry you didn't bring your trunks," she said. "You look like you could use a swim."

"I'd probably drown. I don't have that much time anyway. But it's kind of you to offer."

"Why do you want to talk to me? My book is out of print now, they tell me. It's been remaindered. I don't know what that means exactly, but it doesn't sound nice."

"Are you working on anything else?"

She smiled. "Stu, you don't really think I'm a writer, do you?"

"No," he confessed, "I don't. I had a look at a copy of your book yesterday, and I saw a note in the acknowledgements thanking Ransom Blaisdell for his assistance in the preparation of the manuscript. It was Ransom Blaisdell I wanted to ask you about. How much of the book did he write?"

She laughed musically. "You terrible man, you know perfectly well he wrote the whole damned thing. I can write a check or a shopping list or on a good day even a letter. But I am not capable of writing a book. Ransom interviewed me a few times, did a lot of research on my matches, got my opinions of things and my memories on tape, then wrote the book. I had a cursory look at the manuscript before it went to the publisher. I thought he did a damn good job, by the way. According to our contract, only my name would appear on the dust jacket and the title page, but he would get an acknowledgement inside."

"Why not an 'as told to' credit for Blaisdell? That's more usual these days."

"What a rude question," she said lightly. "I guess I'm a vain person. I wanted people to think that I wrote the book myself. But no one in the publishing business or the book-reviewing business would think that. Certainly not someone like you."

"Of course, you know that Ransom Blaisdell was murdered three months ago."

"Yes, that was very sad," she said. "I was very sorry to hear that. He was a nice man."

"How long did you know him?"

"Well, I only knew him during the time we were working on my book. I hadn't seen him since and never knew him before. He was very polite, very good at his job, very businesslike. I don't think he was really happy with what he was doing. He would have preferred to work on his own projects. But he went about it in a perfectly professional manner. We got along very well."

"How did you happen to get together with Blaisdell?"

She looked at him quizzically. "Just what are you working on here anyway? Obviously it's not me you're interested in but Ransom Blaisdell."

"It would be hard for a man not to be interested in you, Candy. But I am working on something about Ransom Blaisdell, yes."

"Why? He died months ago."

"I think I may have some new angle on the story."

"What new angle?"

"I just think the police may not have looked closely enough into the literary connections of Ranson Blaisdell, that's all. I thought I might talk to a few people who worked with him."

"The police talked to me, very routinely. Blaisdell didn't live very far from here, I understand."

"No."

She made a face of comic suspicion. "Do you think I killed him? Is that it? You'll never take me alive."

"Do you recall who first introduced you to Ransom Blaisdell?"

"I met his agent through a writer friend, and . . . I don't know if I ought to tell you this, really. I don't want to get people needlessly involved."

"I'm a very discreet man, Candy. I'm basically looking for background here. I don't intend to make any irresponsible charges. You can take my word on that."

"And 'background' in reporter talk means you won't quote me by name, right?"

"You got it."

"Okay. It was Arlen Kitchener. He and Blaisdell had the same agent, fellow named Gustavson. Kind of cute."

"Gustavson is cute?"

"You know him?"

"I've talked to him, yes."

"He doesn't appeal to you?"

"No."

"Did you think he would?"

Stu laughed. "Of course not."

"I'm relieved. Men don't understand what women find attractive about other men. It's a very hard thing to explain. Jesus, it's hot out here. Do you mind if I make myself more comfortable?"

Stu swallowed. "I hesitate to ask this, but how do you make yourself more comfortable when wearing nothing but a bikini?"

She smiled. "Let me show you."

"No! Don't!" What the hell is the matter with you, Wellman? he demanded of himself. This beautiful woman wants to throw herself at you, and it's unlike you to turn down such an opportunity.

"Oh, come on, Stu. You're a very attractive man, I'm not bad myself, and we're both well over eighteen."

"Yes, we're adults. But I'm not a consenting adult. I'm—I'm married." You're not married, Wellman. What the hell are you talking about?

She smiled and leaned back. "Okay," she said. "I understand. Oh, I don't really, but at least I can tell myself I'm not being rejected on my merits. Right?"

"Not in the least." What are you doing Wellman? Waves could be crashing against the side of that swimming pool right this very minute. "Getting back to what we were talking about, you say Arlen Kitchener introduced you to Ransom Blaisdell?"

"That's right. Arlen told me that Blaisdell was a good reliable person for the book I wanted to write." She couldn't say it without an amused smirk. "My personal manager at that time got in touch with his agent, Clarence, and finally Randy and I got together. That was what his friends called him, Randy."

"And was he?"

She smiled but didn't answer.

"Did Arlen Kitchener tell you how he happened to know Blaisdell's work?"

"Well, they did have an agent in common."

"Did Kitchener and Blaisdell know each other?"

"I had the feeling that they did."

"Did Blaisdell talk to you about any of his other ghosting jobs?"

"No, Randy was all business. No fun at all, really."

"Did Kitchener use Blaisdell's services himself?"

"What do you mean?"

"Did Kitchener use Blaisdell as a ghost? He told you Blaisdell was reliable, so I wonder how he knew."

"He never said he did. Why would he tell me something like that? We're friends, and we play tennis together a lot, but that's not the kind of thing he'd tell me. And Randy didn't tell me anything about his other ghosting jobs. Neither did his agent, Clarence. Arlen recommended him because he said he knew his work. I don't know how. You should ask him."

"Did you ever meet Marvin Fodor?"

A direct hit. She didn't exactly gasp; she probably didn't turn white as a sheet; and almost certainly she didn't really almost fall out of her lounge. But Stu knew she knew the name and was startled to hear it.

"Yeah, I think I remember him," she said, in a fruitless attempt to seem casual. "A friend of Randy's."

"You met his friends?"

"Only that one. I had dinner at his house one night, and Marv Fodor was there. I think he taught school at the same place as Randy's wife taught."

"Did you only meet him the once?"

"That's something I'm not going to talk about, Stu. Don't press me."

"Knew him pretty well, huh?"

"I said—" The doorbell rang. She seemed pleased at the interruption.

Stu sat at the kitchen table, considering what he'd just learned, or thought he had learned. She must have known Fodor rather well. Did she know he'd been murdered this morning? If she did, hearing his name shouldn't have been such a surprise.

He heard the door opening, a little gasp from Candy, and a loud, unpleasant voice saying, "I want to talk to you, you goddam bitch!"

"I have a guest," she said in a lowered voice, "and you can't walk in here and—"

Stu entered the living room and saw a straggly-haired young man walking through the door.

"Just who the fuck are you?" the newcomer demanded.

"Stu Wellman, Los Angeles *News-Canvas*," said Stu snappily. "And I think your name is Craig Kitchener, right?"

"Yeah, that's right." Craig didn't seem to know what to do. He offered a perfunctory handshake. "I read your column. You ought to review more modern poetry in your paper. Poets hardly have a chance." After a pause, he added, "How do you know who I am?"

"I've seen pictures of you in your father's files in my paper's morgue."

"My father's files, huh? I should have known. You have some interest in my father? That's why you're here?"

"Why would an interest in your father bring me here?"

"What else would bring you here? Candy's literary career?"

"Sure, why not?"

Candy, apparently feeling underdressed suddenly, had put on a short white robe and somewhat recovered her poise. "On the whole," she said, "I think I'd like both of you gentlemen to leave. At once. Not one at a time."

In reply, Craig Kitchener sat down in one of the living room easy chairs. Stu shrugged and followed suit, sitting down in another.

"Maybe we should all have a friendly chat first," he said. "Let's talk about books."

12.

Hollywood Boulevard was still a book lover's paradise if sleazy and depressing in almost every other way. After only about twenty minutes of searching, Rachel came across her first copy of Arlen Kitchener's *The Atlantis Courier*. She pulled it off the shelf and opened it to the flyleaf. It was identified as a first edition and priced at twenty dollars! She reminded herself that prices differed depending on what boulevard you were on. Turning to the half title, though, she found an inscription that partially accounted for the price: "To Michael Armitage, whose friendship the author has always valued. Best wishes, Arlen Kitchener."

Rachel thought about it. Away from Vermilion's she felt no rapport with the literary ghosts—indeed, the whole enterprise seemed faintly ridiculous. She stood there trying to imagine whether the "ghost of a ghost" would consider affixing his signature to a volume the ostensible author had already signed. Maybe the presence of the Kitchener signature would lead Blaisdell to include some other clue, some sarcastic comment perhaps. Or maybe it would scare him off altogether. Maybe signing already signed books was against the rules.

She was fairly sure she could find a cheaper copy—even a book club edition would do—somewhere else, and her finances were not so healthy she would not feel the twenty dollars. But something told her she should acquire it and, to be on the safe side, another copy as well. She paid for the copy, and the supercilious look the clerk gave her implied that he was making an inward comment on her literary tastes. He probably knew the thing was overpriced, but that should only make him faintly embarrassed on behalf of the store, not contemptuous of the customer.

Back on Hollywood Boulevard, she reflected that not all bookstores were as friendly as Uncle Oscar had made Vermilion's.

Going in and out of bookstores, indulging herself in no more purchases except for a $2.25 book-club copy of *The Atlantis Courier*, Rachel managed to fill a few more hours. Occasionally she asked desultory questions about Kitchener and Ransom Blaisdell, but they seemed to get her nowhere. The old guard of book dealers, the lovers of the printed word that Oscar Vermilion had known so well, didn't seem to be around today. Dead or out to lunch.

She saw several other volumes she would have liked to take back to the store to tempt their deceased authors, but the prices charged for most of them on Hollywood Boulevard were more than she would charge even with the autograph. Looking at new and old books tended to put troubling thoughts out of her mind, but they kept surfacing every time she emerged in the bright sunlight.

Rod Wellman was flying in tonight, and she would probably hear from him not too long after Stu picked him up at the airport. She wasn't sure what to say to him or what he expected of her. To complicate matters further, she had agreed to have dinner with Manuel Gonzales. Call him Manny, he'd said. For a loner, she seemed unusually concerned to have someone to talk to all the time, but a dinner with a policeman investigating the murder in her store could hardly be either a pleasant sociable evening or an opportunity to unburden herself. He would be bound to ask about *The Atlantis Courier*. Cops were never off duty. She'd dated one in Tempe, and all he could talk about was giving traffic tickets.

With the time she was supposed to meet Gonzales approaching, Rachel decided to explore one more bookstore. She saw the sign from the corner, half a block down a side street from Hollywood Boulevard. The name of the store was Meegher's and there was a display of science fiction pulp magazines in the window. The name was vaguely familiar, and somehow the pulps struck a responsive chord, too. She entered the store, gently closing the heavy door behind her.

"Hi," said a voice from behind the counter. It emerged from a jungle of white beard that seemed to cover both the face and chest of its wearer, whose massive form filled a leather swivel chair.

"Hello," she said.

"Anything I can help you with?"

"Do you have anything by Arlen Kitchener in stock?"

"I use schlockmeisters like him for firewood. His books, I mean. But you have to realize I regard book-burning as an act of

114

criticism, not censorship. If his books ever get hard to find, I'll start selling them. Harold Robbins, Arthur Hailey, Irving Wallace, all those guys. But I think I'm safe."

"I know you," she said to the blue eyes that peered out above the white beard.

"Do you? I'd like to know you. But don't get me wrong. You have to realize that to know you in the Biblical sense, I would have to turn back the clock some years. Where do you know me from?"

"I can't quite put my finger on when, but I think you must have been a friend of my Uncle Oscar's. And you're a science fiction dealer."

"Little Rachel! I'll be doggoned, Oscar's pretty niece. You have to realize my memory's about all that's in working order now. Even my eyes can barely make you out. Yeah, I used to come in Oscar's all the time, and I sure do remember you. You must have recognized my voice, 'cause I wasn't affecting this foliage the last time I saw you. But I was so good-looking, I was causing accidents in the street. So I started on this beard in the interest of public safety. You never knew me as Meegher, just as Blast-Off. That's what they called me, Blast-Off. It was damn funny in the old days, and it seems pretty corny now, but that's what they still call me, those that are around and calling that is. I was specializing in this stuff long before anybody else was, you know."

"Sci-fi?"

"My stars, don't call it sci-fi. S.f., if you must. Oscar didn't teach you such naughty words, did he? Look, sit down close, and we'll have a talk. I'm practically immobile here. They steal me blind. Not many dealers left from our era. Tell me about what you've been doing."

There was plenty Rachel could tell him without going into ghost signatures. He was surprised she had reopened Vermilion's, and it was obvious he hadn't heard about the murder of Marvin Fodor. He told her he never turned on his radio. "You have to realize, I'm living in the past. Past futures, you might say."

"Did you know Ransom Blaisdell?"

"I knew him well, Rachel. Very well. Old drinking buddy, in fact. Randy wasn't a heavy drinker all the time, like some writers, but when he tied one on, he tied one on. He knew where to tie it, you might say. We talked of real literature and phony literature and bug-eyed monsters. We all have our bug-eyed monsters, but some of them wear business suits. I heard Randy died, poor guy."

"He was a ghostwriter, wasn't he?"

"Thankless calling, that. You have to realize the reason writers write is for recognition. I don't think any writer's really happy with another name on his work. Wouldn't think he'd be any happier with his name on another's work, but that's probably easier to take. Randy wasn't a happy man."

Carefully, Rachael tried to draw the old bookseller out about Ransom Blaisdell. Maybe she could learn something useful.

"Did he ever talk about his ghosting jobs?"

"Oh, yeah. But he never mentioned names, or almost never. Randy was pretty scrupulous about that. He told me some stories, though, without the names. He said he'd written a best-selling novel, a book that must have earned millions, and got paid a pittance for it. I remember the number he quoted me. Seven thousand, seven hundred and fifty. One drunken night, he just kept saying that number over and over and over again. Like a litany almost."

"But he didn't say what book it was?"

"No, no. I remember I made a game out of trying to guess it from him. *Hawaii? Anatomy of a Murder? How to Avoid Probate?* It gave us both a laugh, and I didn't really care what book it was. But he was stuck on that number. Seven thousand, seven hundred and fifty."

"Did he ever mention Arlen Kitchener's name?"

"Rachel, you have to realize we talked about great literature and great trash, but you wouldn't catch us talking about that middle-brow junk. No, indeed."

"Do you have any of Ransom Blaisdell's books here?"

"If you go back among the paperbacks, you might find some s.f. he wrote back in the fifties. Not under his own name, though.

" Let's see, what names did he use? "

The beard shook with laughter.

"Didn't he say anything else about the best-seller he ghosted?"

"You have to realize I didn't encourage him in the subject. I tried to get it off his mind. It was business, and there was nothing he could do about it. He said he had a copy of the manuscript, gave it to a friend for safe-keeping, that it would prove his authorship. But the only answer to that is, so what? He'd made a deal. And Randy always honored deals like that."

"Who did he leave the manuscript with?"

"I don't know. I didn't ask him."

"Who would he have left it with?" she persisted.

"Well, honey, I think your Uncle Oscar would have been the most likely candidate. They were pretty close."

Before the book dealer could ask the obvious question of why she was so interested in all this stuff, Rachel looked at her watch and saw that it was nearly time to meet Manny Gonzales. She said good-bye to Blast-Off Meegher and promised to come back to his shop when she had more time.

As they had arranged, Gonzales picked her up at five-thirty, pulling up in front of the huge Pickwick Bookshop, now part of the B. Dalton chain. She was glad to see him. As night came closer, the surroundings got stranger, a sea of hustlers, religious fanatics, male and female prostitutes, beggars, elderly strollers in conversation with themselves, wild-eyed figures in Army fatigues defying categorization. They walked over the stars of a dead Hollywood. The town had always been socially avant garde in one way or another, but what would long-dead stars like Mae Murray or Lowell Sherman or even Clara Bow think if they saw the boulevard today?

Gonzales surprised her. He did throw a policemanly glance at the two small packages she held in her hand and asked if she'd gotten what she was after.

"Not sure," she smiled.

"How can you not—?" he started, but checked himself. And from that point through a pleasant dinner at a Mexican restaurant—where Gonzales ignored the printed menu and ordered some unlisted Mexico City specialties from the proprietor, who apparently was a relative—he seemed to do his best not to talk like a cop. She was relieved.

As usual, the part of the flight spent taxiing on the ground at L.A. International Airport seemed the longest. Rodney Wellman obeyed the injunction to remain in his seat until the aircraft came to a complete stop. But he hunched over with one hand on the carry-on bag under the seat in front of him, like a runner in the blocks. He had no other luggage, so he could get away in a hurry. Why hurry? He didn't fear keeping Stu waiting, because one way or another he was confident his brother would fail to meet the plane. He'd have to take a cab or try to rent a car or. . . . Damn Los Angeles and its phony people and its genuine smog and its overpriced restaurants. Maybe he should stay on the plane. He wondered if the same plane was going back to Arizona. No, it would be worth it to get Rachel out of this place and back to Tempe where she belonged.

He hoped she was safe but miserable. Her letters were damned uninformative. She might as well not have written at all. It didn't occur to him that his own lack of letters was even less informative.

Out of the plane, he bustled down the long corridor with his single bag. Why was he in such a hurry? It must be Southern California infecting him with its metropolitan frenzy.

As he passed the airport security point, he saw a lean figure half running toward him. It was Stu. He apparently had misjudged his brother.

"Stu," he began, but before he could say more the running figure snatched the bag out of his hand.

"Come on, Roddy, for God's sake, you want me to get a ticket? Let's get a move on." He began sprinting toward the exit of the terminal. Rod managed to follow him with a weary trot. Stu had been a high school trackman who learned journalistic objectivity reporting on his own meets. Rod had never been able to keep up with him.

Stu had thrown the bag into the trunk of his car and was behind the wheel with the motor running when Rod puffed up to the passenger side door. A bored male voice was droning, "The white zone is for immediate loading and unloading of passengers only. There is no parking." In an unsuccessful bid for variety, a female voice repeated the same message. An airport cop was taking a hard look at Stu's car.

Rod dropped into the passenger seat, wheezing, and Stu pulled away from the curb with alacrity.

"You're damned slow, Roddy. Out of shape."

"Don't . . . call . . . me . . . Roddy," his brother managed to get out between heavy breaths. Until they were on the freeway heading toward downtown, he didn't attempt to speak again.

"Stu, I appreciate your meeting me. I really do. But you still drive too fast."

"I'm a busy man, Rod. I've got columns to write, murders to solve."

"Murders to solve? You've switched to the crime beat?"

"Not really. This one's a literary murder. And I found the body."

Rod shook his head as if to clear the cobwebs. "I don't understand. A literary murder. You've taken up writing detective fiction? Is that it?"

"Not writing it, living it. We found this corpse in Vermilion's bookstore, you see."

"We? Vermilion's? Is Rachel involved in this?"

"If you can consider the owner of the store in which the body is found to be involved, I guess you'd have to say she's involved. But it's open to interpretation. It depends on what you mean by involved. The dictionary definition of involved is—"

"Stu, stop running off at the mouth, and tell me the whole story. All of it."

"Sure, Rod," Stu replied. He had no intention of telling his brother quite all of the story, but he could tell him the parts of it his earthbound brain could comprehend, that is omitting the origin of the signed *Atlantis Courier*. By the time they were ensconced in Stu's apartment, each holding a drink that was highly desired but really not needed, his brother was incredulously asking him why he had turned down Candy Helms.

"It seems so unlike you, Stu."

Stu was uncharacteristically embarrassed. He didn't really know why, and what suspicions he had he wasn't about to share with his brother. He moved on quickly and soon reached the point of Craig Kitchener's arrival at the home of Candy Helms.

"We had a long chat, the three of us. I convinced them they should cooperate with me at least up to a point, but it wasn't easy. Appropriate to the personnel, our conversation was quite a bit like a tennis match. But this was what I was able to put together.

"Candy Helms is quite a friendly girl. I won't say that every man in Southern California has been to bed with her, but certainly everyone I've come across. Among her lovers were both the old novelist Arlen Kitchener and the son Craig Kitchener. Now Candy is a good-time girl who's able to enter into lots of relationships without getting too uptight about commitment and things like that. But with the elder Kitchener, she was more serious for a while. Apparently he couldn't just have a good time—he was of the old school and felt a measure of hypocrisy was expected of him, so he promised her that he would divorce his wife to marry her. If he hadn't started talking that way, she would have been happy with just sex. But when he did, she began to see visions of being the wife of a best-selling novelist, and started to like the idea. Arlen Kitchener, of course, did not come through, probably had no intention of doing so or (to give him the benefit of the doubt) just came to his senses, and broke off their relationship, at least the sexual part of it. Amiable by habit, Candy took it like a good sport and continued to play tennis with him. Still does, in fact. But deep down she had a certain bitterness about the way he'd treated her."

Rod Wellman nodded sagely. "It festers when you submerge it. It's bound to. It's better to let it out."

"Well, she finally did let it out, but in a poisonous sort of form. Enter another lover. After Arlen Kitchener had put her onto Ransom Blaisdell as a reliable ghost for her memoirs—without, of course, mentioning the fact that he had himself used Blaisdell's services on *The Atlantis Courier*—she also got to know Marvin Fodor, the guy that turned up dead in Rachel's bookstore. Got to know him very well. He was a friend of Blaisdell's and a teaching colleague of Blaisdell's wife. And you are no doubt aware, Rod, bed tends to make people indiscreet. Blaisdell, in good ghostly fashion, had been sworn to secrecy over his involvement in *The Atlantis Courier*. At first, not even his wife knew. But he was bitter over reverses in his own literary career and developed a compulsion to tell people how he had written a best-seller and gotten stiffed on the payment for it."

"He wasn't paid?"

"Oh, he was paid all right, but to his way of thinking, he wasn't

120

paid enough. Unfortunately for him, the whole thing was work for hire. Once it was published, the royalties and the movie rights and everything else accrued to Arlen Kitchener. He didn't get anything out of it at all. I don't know how much he got paid, but it's easy to imagine it wasn't enough. So, as I say, he developed this compulsion. You shrinks know all about compulsions, of course. A good example of compulsive behavior is taking a night flight all of a sudden to chase an old girl friend who—"

"Stu, I'm getting a compulsion to break your neck. Get off the editorial page and back on the news pages, will you?"

Stu raised his glass in salute. "That's very good, Rod. Anyway, Blaisdell didn't go out and tell the *Times* or anything like that, but he couldn't resist telling his wife and then his closest friend. This set off what we'll refer to as the bedroom grapevine, or maybe the old ball network. In a moment of intimacy, the friend, Marvin Fodor, apparently let slip to Candy Helms the information that Blaisdell had given him, about the ghosting of Kitchener's book.

"Sometime early this year, Candy Helms started laying Arlen Kitchener's son, Craig."

"A transparent attempt to get back at the old man. She sounds like a real bitch."

"I don't know about that," said Stu, feeling oddly defensive on the tennis player's behalf. "She seems like a nice person to me."

"A hooker with a heart of gold?"

"She's no hooker, Rod. Nobody pays her."

"You just never got to the point where she offers her bill. Look, Stu, whether she knows it or not, she started sleeping with the son as a way of getting back at the father."

"And you've never met any of them. I didn't know psychology was such an exact science."

"Okay, okay. She's a nice lady, and she picked young Kitchener because he was the nearest available. Then what happened?"

Stu snickered. "I don't know how this is going to sound, Rod, but really she's a very nice person."

"Don't tell me. She tells Craig his old man's book was ghostwritten, right? And that sets the whole mess in motion. And you're telling me she wasn't being malicious when she did it?"

"Well, there might have been a slight touch of malice to it. But

121

she had no way of knowing how traumatic this would prove to the kid, especially since the ghostwritten novel is the only book by his father that Craig Kitchener admired. If it turns out to be a phony, what little bit of respect exists between father and son goes down the tubes. But she didn't realize that.

"Anyway, when she told him, presumably in another moment of intimacy, he got mad, claimed he didn't believe her. Actually, he half did and half didn't. He couldn't be sure. Once she saw what damage she'd caused, she tried to backtrack, withdraw what she'd said, convince him she'd made it up just to hurt him. But it was too late. Craig became determined to find out who the ghostwriter was, information Candy wasn't about to pass along once she saw how he was affected by what had been revealed up to then. Anyway, he stormed out of the house, determined to find the truth. Not long after that, Ransom Blaisdell was murdered."

"And the son killed him?"

"He says he didn't."

"Naturally. What would you expect him to say?"

"I don't see a motive for the son to kill Blaisdell, do you? And anyway, at that point he apparently didn't know who the ghostwriter was. He and Candy both claim that she didn't tell him. If he found out the story was true, I can more easily imagine him killing his father. Who had betrayed Craig, after all? Not Ransom Blaisdell."

"Maybe he did it to protect his father."

"Somehow I can't imagine him going to that extreme. I can see that love and hate for his father may be inextricably mixed in this kid, and that angry as he was, he might want to cover up the truth. But to commit murder just to protect his father's reputation? Remember that even if the story came out, his father hadn't done anything illegal. He wasn't in danger of dying or even going to jail. Would Craig put so much stock in just his father's good name?"

"You never know. People's minds have more possibilities than a layman can ever guess."

"Layman, huh? You always did like to call me names, brother."

"Who do you think killed Blaisdell and Fodor, Stu?"

"Somebody who didn't want Blaisdell to talk out of turn and

reveal his authorship of *The Atlantis Courier*. Maybe Arlen Kitchener himself. If his son wouldn't kill to protect his reputation, Arlen himself might. Something happened shortly before his death to make the killer fear Blaisdell would talk. And his death followed that of Oscar Vermilion by only a few days. There may be a connection there."

"Why should there be a connection with Vermilion? I don't see it."

"Blaisdell used to frequent Vermilion's store. But then so did half the writers in Hollywood." Stu stopped there. He didn't want to say anything at this point about ghosts and phantom signatures.

"Would anybody else have enough of a motive to kill over *The Atlantis Courier*? Maybe Kitchener's wife?"

"Or his agent."

"I don't see that he'd have enough to lose." Rod yawned. "I haven't slept in I don't know how long. And I didn't come here to play—wait a minute. I don't understand why Craig Kitchener picked today to storm into Candy Helms' house and start calling her names."

"I think it's a variation on the killing-the-messenger syndrome, Roddy. He'd first heard about the ghosting from her, and he thought of her as the person who started the whole mess, even though she really had very little to do with it. And I don't think he wants the truth of his father's use of ghosts to come out publicly. He wanted to use it against his father in the happy family circle, not make it common coin for the great wide world. He wanted to make sure she kept quiet. And he might have been afraid his father killed Blaisdell and Fodor."

"What do you mean he might have wanted to use it in the family circle?"

"That's another little piece of information I picked up today. Craig Kitchener made an anonymous phone call to his father, saying he was Ransom Blaisdell. Wanted to scare the old man."

Rod heaved a sigh. "Stu, I would be much more effective in my profession if I were as good at digging information out of people as you are."

Unable to deal with the compliment, Stu ignored it. "He got

the information from Marvin Fodor shortly before he died, and used it in a phone call to scare his father. I think he's sorry he did it now, and that's why he was so anxious to confess it to somebody."

"He'd talked to Fodor, though."

"Yes. Only a day or so before he died. But he claims he didn't kill him."

"I don't know about that," said Rod, yawning again. "Damn it, Stu, this is all very interesting, but I came here to see Rachel. Do you think we could go over there and . . . ?"

"At this hour? Have you looked at the clock? Why don't you sack out now, and you can see Rachel in the morning."

"I guess that would be better," the psychologist agreed. Knowing he could hope for nothing better in his brother's apartment, he slipped his shoes off, stretched out on the sofa where he sat, and went to sleep.

Stu looked at his brother jealously. He could still go to sleep at will, just like when he was a kid. Leaving his brother snoring, Stu left the apartment.

13.

Stu was rather pleased that a police officer asked him who he was and what he was doing there almost as soon as he arrived at Vermilion's. It showed the L.A.P.D. was watching out for Rachel. From the back of the building, he saw that the light was still on in the upstairs apartment. The policeman escorted him upstairs, where Manuel Gonzales answered the door.

"You keep long hours, Detective," Stu said smilingly. Why did the cop look kind of embarrassed when he said that, he wondered. "Actually, I'm glad to see you. I have some information I think might help you."

Not about to tell Stu that he was technically off duty, Gonzales led the reporter into the apartment and asked Rachel's permission to have their discussion there. Stu thought Rachel looked a little uncomfortable, too, and he sensed the lightbulb flickering over his head. Apparently, brother Rod was not his only competition in the Rachel stakes. No, that wasn't what he meant.

Stu told both of them everything he had learned. As with Rod, he omitted any reference to Rachel's peculiar talent, but he held back nothing else.

The policeman turned to Rachel. "What about those two books you picked up in Hollywood? Were either of them helpful?"

She shook her head wearily. "I really don't know, Detective Gonzales. I'll have to have a better look at them and call you in the morning."

Gonzales nodded. "Okay. You've given me plenty to chew on, and plenty of people to talk to. I advise you to be very careful, Miss Hennings."

Stu wanted to tell them they didn't have to be so formal for his benefit.

"If someone did commit this crime with the idea of submerging the truth about *The Atlantis Courier*," the detective went on, "you might very well be in danger. Especially if this manuscript you told me about really exists and is still hidden somewhere in the store. I'll keep a man watching this place, and if anything suspicious happens, you must call on him. If you can't reach me when you call tomorrow, leave a message and I'll return your call."

The detective left.

"Looks like a young Ramon Novarro, doesn't he?" Rachel remarked.

Maintaining his usual bantering tone with some effort, Stu countered, "Ramon Novarro was gay."

"He isn't."

"How do you know?"

She grinned mischievously. "I really don't. Stu, if you could see the naked jealousy on your face."

"Bullshit!" he said. "My jealousy is fully clothed. What's it to me if you go for Valentino clones? Actually, I think he looks more like Ricardo Cortez."

"Who's Ricardo Cortez?"

"Gee, when you mentioned Ramon Novarro, I thought you were a fellow movie buff."

"Did Rod get in okay?"

"Yeah, he's fine. And don't worry. I won't tell him about Erik Estrada."

"Who's Erik Estrada?" She laughed. "Seriously, Stu, we did have dinner and a nice chat and he wasn't on duty when you got here, but beyond that . . ."

"Okay, okay no excuses necessary." Of course they weren't necessary. If, Stu told himself, he was turning down other opportunities because he'd fallen in love with somebody he had no business falling in love with, that was his problem. Back to business. "What was that Gonzales said about a manuscript?"

"An old friend of Uncle Oscar's told me that Blaisdell might have left a copy of his manuscript of *The Atlantis Courier* somewhere for safe keeping. Maybe with Uncle Oscar. That could have been what our burglar was looking for. It may also have been one reason why Fodor arranged to meet the killer at the store. They may have been planning to search for it again."

"Must be well hidden if it exists. I can't see it being a big deal now, though, with the authorship of *The Atlantis Courier* out in the open. What are the two books Gonzales referred to?"

She took the two copies of *The Atlantis Courier* out of a bag on her coffee table.

"I thought I'd manufacture some more evidence," she said. "Let's take them downstairs to the shop."

"Okay."

They descended the stairs. She switched on the lights in the shop.

"Will this bring the cop running?" Stu wondered.

"I told him I might be working in here tonight, so he won't suspect a burglar or anything."

"Might be better if he did."

"No one can get in here without his knowing, Stu. You found that out."

She sat at Uncle Oscar's round table, picked up a pen, and opened the copy of *The Atlantis Courier* already inscribed by Kitchener on the flyleaf. She took a few deep breaths. Stu watched her, fascinated.

With a jerking motion, she picked up the pen and with an almost violent stroke scratched out Arlen Kitchener's name. Then, quickly, the name of Ransom Blaisdell raced across the page under the obliterated signature. It was obviously the same signature they had seen before, but it seemed more angular and hurried. There was something angry-looking about it, as though the presence of Kitchener's name on the page was an even greater affront to Blaisdell.

Rachel closed the cover and began to reach for the book club copy of the novel.

Stu said softly, "Wait."

He licked his lips. It was warm in the store, but something was making him shiver. In a slightly cracking voice, he said, "He'd like to help us. Maybe we can ask him a question."

Rachel looked dubious but continued looking straight at Stu, ready to cooperate as far as possible with whatever he had in mind.

"Right to the point," said Stu softly, "let's ask him who killed him."

"How do we do that?"

Stu shrugged. "You're the medium. I'm just a visiting skeptic.

You pick up the pen and we'll just concentrate on the question. Who killed you, Randy? Okay?"

"Okay."

She picked up the pen, and for a few moments they concentrated with all their power on the question. But nothing happened.

"It's not working," she said at last. "Maybe all he can do is sign his name. Other information is against the rules."

"He could cross out Kitchener's name. That was more than just signing his name."

"Maybe he doesn't know who killed him."

"Sure, he knows!" said Stu. Suddenly he felt as if she were the skeptic and he the true believer. "There was nobody else in the room with him when he was clobbered. And he'll have had plenty of time to think about it since—"

"But who killed him has nothing to do with the book."

"You don't think so?"

"Not directly. Maybe if we asked him something that had to do with the book itself."

Stu sighed. "Okay, Rachel. I'll tell you what I'd like to know. It's something Blaisdell could tell us, that we presumably could check, and that you'd have no way of knowing. If it turns out to be accurate, it would be further proof Blaisdell's autograph is real. I'd like to know how much he was paid for the ghosting job on *The Atlantis Courier*. Can he tell us that, do you think?"

Rachel gave a small shrug. "Your guess is as good as mine. I doubt it, though. It just doesn't feel right, too much like table rapping. I just don't feel like a spirit medium, Stu."

He looked at her suspiciously. "Rachel, what's so funny. I see a giggle ready to burst forth."

"It's just that the question you started to ask Blaisdell happens to be one I might already know the answer to. I'm not sure, but I might." She told him about Blast-Off Meegher and Blaisdell's drunken repetition of the figure $7,750.

"Did you tell Gonzales about this?"

"Yes, when I told him about the possible existence of Blaisdell's manuscript. But it's hardy solid evidence. It might have referred to some other best-seller he ghosted. Still, if he was so obsessed about being cheated by Kitchener, I'd say there was a pretty good chance that was the one."

Stu looked around the shop, as if searching for some physical manifestation of Rachel's ghosts, and said, "Well, you hear that, Randy? Does she have the right amount?"

Rachel drew another deep breath, let it out slowly. She picked up the pen again and reopened the book club volume to the flyleaf. After a moment she wrote,

$7,750!

RANSOM BLAISDELL

"There we are," said Stu. "But who wrote the figure above the signature? You or Blaisdell?"

"It looks like his handwriting," said Rachel. "Maybe we collaborated."

14. "Detective Gonzales," said Clarence Gustavson, with uncharacteristic somberness, "I'm afraid our little deception has gotten away from us. I'm ready to be completely candid with you, tell you the whole story. It would be beneficial for us to limit the publicity on this as much as possible, but I don't know if there is anything you can do about that. At any rate, I will tell you the complete truth, and if anyone else has lied to you in order to keep this otherwise harmless deception from you, well, I can only hope you'll be understanding."

Manny Gonzales looked across the agent's desk and said nothing, confident that the man he was questioning was about to come to the point. No reason to hurry him.

"To begin with, it's true that my client Arlen Kitchener did not write *The Atlantis Courier*. That is the only novel to appear under his name that he did not write in its entirety. The true author of the novel was Ransom Blaisdell, also my client."

"Why didn't you make this known during the investigation of Blaisdell's murder, Mr. Gustavson?"

Gustavson spread his hands. His face had an expression of comic ruefulness. "I think my next line is something like, 'Well, Officer, I didn't think there was any connection.' And I really didn't think so. That is, I don't really think that Blaisdell's ghosting activities had anything to do with his death. But I did have reason to think there might be some such connection, or it would appear that there was, and I didn't say anything, it's true. But now I realize the deception just can't continue. It has to end. Like all good things and, thankfully, most bad things, eh?"

The agent seemed to be choosing his words so carefully that it actually began to seem doubtful he would get to the point without prodding.

"Please go on, Mr. Gustavson."

"Why don't I start at the beginning?"

"Please start somewhere," said Gonzales, a bit testily. He didn't like the tone he heard in his voice. His usual style was low-key and sympathetic, and that usually got more information than hostility.

"I met Arlen Kitchener when we served together in World War II. We both wanted to be writers, but I guess I didn't have what it took to do it. After the war, I worked in New York as an editor—well, a reader is more like it—for one of the publishing houses, then joined one of the larger literary agencies in a position of similar responsibility and power. I often got the important task of going for sandwiches.

"The turning point for me as an agent came when I introduced my old friend Arlen to the agency when he was trying to peddle his first novel in 1949. I continued to handle Arlen's work. After his first best-seller in 1955, he got offers to do movie work and decided to move west. I followed him, quit the old agency, and set up my own here. I have been very, very successful. A lot of my income derives from Arlen's work, but I have other good clients, too. I really want to do nothing at all to hurt Arlen. That's why telling this is so difficult for me."

"It's your duty as a citizen, Mr. Gustavson. Just go right ahead."

"In the spring of 1969, Arlen came to me and said he was in trouble. He's always had almost unlimited supplies of energy and has always completed his writing projects right on deadline. But this time the poor guy had burned himself out. He said he had a bad case of writer's block and didn't think he'd be able to deliver his next novel on time that fall. By that time, we were selling the damned things on the basis of a title or a sentence describing the plot. We still do it that way. We've been so reliable, nobody ever worries we won't come through with the required product on time.

"Actually, I think it wasn't really writer's block. There just weren't enough hours in the day. He was doing the script of his novel *The Hungerford Inquiry*, and at the same time he was working on a three-act play and several magazine articles for big markets. The play was a turkey, by the way, closed on Broadway in 1970 after just four performances. You probably wonder why they call them turkeys."

"Not really."

"Plays that opened on Thanksgiving were invariably expected to close. So in the theater they call them turkeys."

"Mr. Gustavson, please."

"Now they call people turkeys. You look like you're about to call me one. I know I keep changing the subject, but this is really painful for me. Anyway, all Arlen had for his novel was a title, *The Atlantis Courier*, and a one-paragraph summary. Arlen was in a panic. I told him not to worry, that the publisher would understand and give us an extension, but he seemed worried about his reputation as a writing machine being ruined. In soft tones, I suggested a ghostwriter."

Gustavson chuckled. "You know, I think Arlen's initial reaction to that is a measure of his basic integrity. He ranted and raved and stormed and raged and said he'd never heard of such a thing. He got so red in the face, I'd have been afraid he'd drop dead of a heart attack, if he didn't always keep himself in such good physical shape. Once he calmed down, I told him that another client of mine, Ransom Blaisdell, could do the job quickly and well and was very discreet. No one needed to know he was the real author. Finally, Arlen agreed.

"Blaisdell, to give him his due, was both fast and competent. In some ways, he was a better writer than Arlen, though it's crummy of me to say that. He certainly could do a fine job of imitating another man's style. He finished the work by the end of summer. Arlen read it and edited it, rewriting some parts and adding his own touches. He sent it on to me in a freshly typed script, looking like the usual Kitchener product, and I sent it on to the publisher. Everybody was happy. The damn thing even got good reviews, and that doesn't usually happen with an Arlen Kitchener novel. Critics don't like writers who are too successful. Don't ask me why. Anyway, I think the good reviews as much as anything got Arlen's goat, and he was determined never to use a ghostwriter again. Ever since then he's turned out his own product his old reliable way and gotten his old reliable lousy reviews."

The agent shook with nervous laughter. Gonzales continued to sit impassively. There had to be more than this to justify the agent's buildup.

"Now we're getting to some things I'm not too proud of, but I hope you'll realize I was trying to protect a friend. From the first, Arlen was worried that Blaisdell would let the cat out of the bag with regard to the authorship of *The Atlantis Courier,* and that would ruin Arlen's reputation. He wanted to be assured Blaisdell had plenty of work, even recommended him to other people, without telling them his recommendation was based on first-hand experience with Blaisdell's services. I assured him that Blaisdell was a pro, would never talk about a ghosting job, and for all I knew that was the pure truth. But Blaisdell wasn't the close-mouthed pro I thought he was.

"On March 14 of last year, late at night, I got a call from Arlen. He was in a panic again. Edgar Ferris had been going through Oscar Vermilion's papers—old Vermilion had just died and Edgar was his lawyer. He found some notes for an autobiography Vermilion was writing, and the manuscript included a veiled hint that *The Atlantis Courier* had been written by somebody other than Arlen Kitchener. Edgar had told Arlen about it, and Arlen of course had vehemently denied it. If you talk to Edgar, he can verify this. I don't imagine he was even questioned at the time of Blaisdell's death, since there was no reason for anybody to think there was any connection between Vermilion's death and Blaisdell's.

"Anyway, Arlen was worried. He figured that if Blaisdell had told Vermilion, who knew who else he might have told? I told Arlen not to worry, that there would be no problems, that Vermilion was just guessing. But Arlen said he was going to see Blaisdell the next day."

"The day Blaisdell was murdered," said Gonzales.

"At that time, he owned a car very much like the one that neighbors described as being parked in front of the Blaisdell house on the day of the crime. He got rid of it a few days later."

"Didn't that seem suspicious to you at the time, Mr. Gustavson?"

"I swear to you," the agent said, "that I never thought Arlen Kitchener killed Ransom Blaisdell. And despite everything that's happened, I still don't. That is the honest truth, Detective Gonzales. Of course, I know I should have told the police everything I knew at the time. But I thought Arlen was innocent, and I didn't want the truth about *The Atlantis Courier* to come out any more than he did. So I didn't say anything. If that makes me guilty of

133

some kind of offense, well, I'll be glad to take my medicine like a man."

"I can imagine any one of a number of offenses that it might constitute, Mr. Gustavson. But let's not worry about that for the moment. I just want the truth. Did Blaisdell and Kitchener know each other before the time Blaisdell did the novel?"

"As far as I know, they had never met before that time." The agent swallowed. "There's a bit more I have to tell you. Arlen called me that afternoon, told me he'd been to Blaisdell's place but found the man dead when he got there. I advised him to keep quiet, since there was nothing to connect him to Blaisdell. I guess that makes my position even worse."

"Yes, sir. You could say that. Why are you opening up about all this now?"

"Two men are dead. And that reporter Wellman was poking around, trying to establish a connection between the murder of Fodor and *The Atlantis Courier*. I don't know what's going on or who's behind these crimes, but I just couldn't keep quiet any longer. And I feel sure Arlen will feel the same way, be happy to tell you everything he knows. We did our best to keep the secret of *The Atlantis Courier*, but now it seems bound to come out. And anyway, it's wrong to obstruct a murder investigation. We did it before, and we don't want to do it again."

Gonzales was getting tired of Gustavson's jocular manner. He seemed the kind of guy who'd be cracking jokes no matter what the circumstances, kind of like that reporter, Wellman. But there was one more question to ask before he could get out of there.

"Did you ever have any intimation that Blaisdell may have kept a rough draft of the novel to prove his authorship?"

"The normal procedure would be to destroy it, in a case like this where secrecy was involved. I supose he might discreetly have kept it. I don't know."

"If he had, finding the manuscript and destroying it might have been important to someone wanting to conceal the real authorship of *The Atlantis Courier*."

The agent shrugged. "Yes, I suppose so. It surely would mean nothing to find it now, though. The original authorship is admitted. Its only value now would be to a manuscript dealer. I can see that it might have a certain curiosity value, like Clifford Irving's autobiography of Howard Hughes, but I hardly think it would be a threat to Arlen or anyone else, do you?"

Gonzales stood up.

"Thank you for the information, Mr. Gustavson. We'll be talking to you again. And if you find out anything more, you must notify me immediately."

The bulky agent rose from his chair. "I will, Detective Gonzales. I've learned my lesson, believe me. No more obstructing."

"And no more being accessory after the fact to homicide, either," Gonzales couldn't resist saying.

The agent quivered slightly. "I hardly think I've been guilty of that."

Gonzales smiled slightly and nodded to the agent. He left the office.

Rod Wellman had awakened at seven A.M. to the smell of coffee and frying bacon.

"Up and at 'em, Roddy," he had heard Stu say. "If you want wheels today, you'll have to come to the paper with me and then take the car from there. And you'll have a hell of a time finding your way around Southern California without wheels. Where are you going today? Disneyland? Knott's berry farm?"

"You know where I'm going. I have to see her."

"The store opens at ten. Better not go before then. She might be worn out and needing her sleep."

"What makes you think so?"

"Oh, I don't know. Finding bodies in your store can be a kind of draining experience, that's all."

"Won't you need the car during the day?"

"I can use one of the paper's cars on their business. It's no problem."

Now, midmorning, Rod was having his first look at Vermilion's. He was not a big fan of used book stores. The pervasive dust had a tendency to get up his nose and make him sneeze. What would he say to her? He wasn't quite sure. How could he convince her to leave this and come back to Tempe with him? Of course, he knew there was nothing he could say really. Whether she would do it or not depended solely on whether she missed Arizona and was sick of this Southern California smog. There was no real argument he could make. Only offer his presence there to let her know his concern, to let her know the option was still open.

There was nothing he could say, so why did he stand looking into the window and thinking about his sales pitch?

He raised his fist to knock on the door. But wait a minute. This was a place of business. He could just open the door and walk right in.

He opened the door, stepped in to the sound of a jingling bell, closed it behind him. He had his first glimpse of Rachel Hennings in all these many weeks. She was standing there at the end of the aisle of books, in her usual uniform of blouse and blue jeans. She looked happy to see him.

"Hello, Rod," she said, smiling.

Dr. Rodney Wellman opened his mouth to speak and sneezed mightily.

"Bless you," she said, touching his arm. He seemed to have an expression of pain on his face. He sneezed again, turning his face away, bending his knees.

Between sneezes, he managed to say, "You should always bend your knees when you sneeze. It's the d-d-d-d——"

"Bless you. The book dust? Come on, let me take you upstairs to my apartment. How was the flight from Phoenix?"

Arlen Kitchener looked pale behind his tan. "Yes, Detective Gonzales, that is the truth. I was at Ransom Blaisdell's house the day he died. I did dispose of my car shortly thereafter. I know it is difficult for you to believe that disposing of my car was something I was planning to do anyway . . ."

"Especially considering that you found Blaisdell's body and failed to report it to the police."

"I didn't want the authorship of *The Atlantis Courier* to become public knowledge. I still don't, but now I don't see what I can possibly do to prevent it. At that time, there was no way that

Blaisdell and I could be connected, except of course through our common agent." Kitchener snapped off the last words bitterly.

"And where were you at the time Marvin Fodor was killed?"

"I already told you that."

"You don't want to change your—"

"Change my story? Is that what you were about to say? I won't change it because it isn't a story. It's the truth. I was here at home working, and my wife Sarah can attest to that fact. I am not a criminal. I have killed no one, and I have done nothing dishonest. Because of fear, I have withheld some information that I ought to have reported, but now I am prepared to cooperate fully with the constituted authorities. I don't know what more than that I can do."

When the policeman had left, Arlen sat staring at the type-writer and the blank page that had never before looked quite so blank. He had called Candy Helms that morning for a tennis date, but she had said she wasn't feeling well. It was a byword of his professional life that he never spent a moment of wasted time. Time not spent writing or sleeping or eating or exercising was spent in research, both in written sources and in social inter-course with human sources. All time must be spent in improving or maintaining the body or mind, or doing the work that brought him fame and fortune. But at that moment, he could do nothing productive, only stare at the blank page in the typewriter.

Sarah brought him a glass of iced tea. He looked at her silently worrying face. It amazed him that they had not discussed the matter, that he had not given her any direct account of whatever it was that was bothering him. Even now he had difficulty knowing what to say, but he had to say something.

He reached out for the glass. It felt cool to the touch. He said, "My son hates me."

It may have been a good popular novelist's narrative hook, but it was a dreadfully incompetent way to start this conversation.

"He doesn't, Arlen," she said.

"He does, and perhaps he should." With the white-knuckled concentration of a poor public speaker forced onto the podium, he told her as much as he could of the story. How much of it she already knew or had guessed, he had no idea.

Stu spend most of the morning trying to get Clarence Gustavson on the phone. Most times, he was told by Gustavson's secretary that the agent was in conference. Finally, late in the morning, he got through.

"I was hoping there was one additional piece of information you could give me for my article, Mr. Gustavson."

"I've been giving myself away in pieces all morning to our friends in the local gendarmerie," the agent said ruefully. "I doubt that one more bit of information will kill me."

"Please tell me the exact price that Arlen Kitchener paid Ransom Blaisdell for ghost writing his book."

The agent sounded puzzled. "Why would you want to publish that?"

"I don't want to publish it. I just want to know."

"Believe me, the figure won't impress you. By current standards, it was the merest pittance. Especially for somebody writing a sure best-seller. Actually, Randy wasn't the best of businessmen. He could have gotten a bit more."

"What was the figure?"

"It was $18,000."

After a surprised pause, Stu said, "That doesn't sound bad."

"We thought it was fair. Of course, it's all relative."

Stu was puzzled when he put down the phone. Of course, there was no reason to expect the two figures to gibe. Rachel's information source didn't strike him as all that reliable, and thinking Blaisdell confirmed the figure from beyond the grave put too much strain on Stu's belief in ghosts. And yet . . . maybe it was time to try again to talk to the ghostwriter's widow. It meant another drive to the Valley, but at least the *News-Canvas* vehicles had air conditioning.

He picked up the phone and dialed the widow's number.

15.

Edgar Ferris nodded magisterially. "Yes, I can verify what Clarence Gustavson told you. Of course, you must understand that I had no notion that item in Oscar Vermilion's autobiography had anything to do with any police investigation, or I would have immediately come forward with the information."

Gonzales, seated in a chair in the attorney's office that was both too low and too soft and made him feel vaguely ridiculous, said, "The entry didn't say who had written *The Atlantis Courier?*"

"No, it just designated the ghostwriter by the initials G. S. I suppose Oscar didn't want to reveal something, even posthumously, that he had been told in confidence, so he invented the initials to cover the person's real name. It was not unlike a blind item in a gossip column, though most of Oscar's memoir was hardly in that category. He didn't mind calling Arlen Kitchener by name, though. I imagine he felt hiring someone to write your book for you was a form of unethical practice."

"Probably. But why G. S.? That suggests the ghost might have been someone other than Blaisdell. Do you know anyone by those initials?"

"No. But I suspect it was a theatrical reference, the abbreviation for George Spelvin."

The policeman looked blank, so Ferris explained. "When an actor appears in two roles in a play, the second is often credited in the program as George Spelvin. Oscar probably liked the idea of using that for an alias."

"And you notified Kitchener when you found this?"

"Yes. He was my client and I thought he should know the accusation had been made."

"And he denied it?"

"Oh, yes. Vehemently."

"Did you believe him?"

The lawyer shrugged his beefy shoulders. "I chose to believe him. It was not a matter of deep concern to me. And when the murder of Blaisdell occurred, I had no reason to connect it with the item in Oscar's memoirs."

"No, I can see that. Who has this manuscript of Mr. Vermilion's now?"

"His heir."

"Rachel Hennings?"

"No, no, she just inherited the bookshop. I mean his son, Daniel Vermilion, Miss Hennings' cousin. If you want to look at the manuscript, I suggest you speak to him. I'm sure he'll be happy to cooperate with you, provided he's kept it of course."

"You think he might have destroyed it?"

Ferris half smiled. "Young Vermilion is not noted for his literary interests. He may have converted the manuscript to firewood for all I know. Actually, though, I seriously doubt you'll find anything much more in there than what I've told you. It was just a brief reference."

"Mr. Ferris, was there any other material in that manuscript that could be used for, uh, different purposes than Mr. Vermilion intended?"

"What do you mean? Do you mean blackmail? Are you considering that as a motive for one or more of these crimes?"

"Not necessarily. But I think the possibility can't be ignored completely. Was there anything like that?"

Ferris shook his head. "Absolutely not. Oscar Vermilion was a kind man, not at all malicious, not at all given to gathering dirt on people. The item on *The Atlantis Courier* was the only thing there I felt impelled to warn anyone about. And in any case, Daniel Vermilion, though I probably ought not to speak quite so freely about a client, hasn't the brains for such an operation. The morals perhaps, but never the brains."

"Do you recall if there was any other manuscript in Vermilion's papers? The manuscript of a novel perhaps?"

"No, I don't think Oscar ever imagined himself a potential novelist."

"I meant a novel by someone else. By a friend of his."

Ferris raised an eyebrow. "You're thinking of the original manuscript of *The Atlantis Courier* perhaps? No, it wasn't there. And believe me, I would have noticed if it had been."

Gonzales nodded and with a desperate attempt at grace extricated himself from the chair. "Thank you, Mr. Ferris, you've been very helpful. Now, where can I reach Daniel Vermilion?"

Estelle Blaisdell was a small woman with birdlike limbs, thin to the vanishing point. She showed no reluctance to let Stu into her cluttered living room, and she offered him a cup of coffee and a sweetroll, but she seemed to be doing it all by rote. She struck him as someone who had lost interest in most things.

He noticed a bookshelf on the wall that held an amazingly eclectic mixture of titles, paperback and hardback, fiction and nonfiction, from children's books to pornography. Among them were the autobiography signed by Candy Helms and *The Atlantis Courier*. Some—not many—had Ransom Blaisdell's name on their spines as author.

Could he actually have written all of these things? If so, must have been a very busy man, not to mention a fast typist.

"They're all his," said Estelle Blaisdell, as if she had heard the unspoken question. "Including *The Atlantis Courier,* as I guess most of the world knows by now."

She stared into her coffee. "Do they have any idea who killed poor Marvin, do you think? They've been here again and again, asking me all kinds of questions, but I can't tell if they know anything or not."

"Was Marvin Fodor your husband's closest friend?"

"Oh, I suppose he was. Randy didn't have much time for friends. Actually I knew Marv first. At school. At the high school. We taught there together for years."

Stu raised an eyebrow. It was hard to imagine this frail lady as a teacher.

"Oh, yes," she said, reading his mind again. "I taught. And I know how I appear to you now. A woman afraid of her own shadow who couldn't handle working with the savage American teenager. Well, I wasn't always this way. I don't know if you remember the riot at Hardisty High, three years ago."

"Certainly," said Stu. It had been an ugly and well-publicized affair.

"I was seriously injured in that horror, Mr. Wellman. Several

141

broken bones. When I was ready to go back to school, physically ready that is, I just couldn't face it. Psychologically. Marv was very angry about what happened to me. And when he realized that Randy could have been a rich man from *The Atlantis Courier,* knowing how much easier that would have made things on me, that made him angrier and angrier. From the time Randy died, the whole question of *The Atlantis Courier* became an obsession with Marv. He was determined that the truth should be known, and that I should get something out of Kitchener. I didn't feel as strongly. It was a job, the kind of work Randy did for a living. It may not have been the most equitable situation in the world, but that was the way things were."

"Mrs. Blaisdell, do you know how much your husband was paid for ghosting *The Atlantis Courier?*"

She shook her head. "No, I never was involved in the business parts of Randy's operation. I never knew how much he got for what job. In the case of *The Atlantis Courier,* I didn't even know what he was working on. It was such an exceptionally secret kind of operation, he wasn't even supposed to tell me, though he did in time, when it started eating away at him."

"But he never mentioned a specific price?"

"No, not that I can remember. I think Randy was perfectly happy in what he was doing as long as my income was a cushion. But when I got hurt, money pressures on him became greater."

She narrated all this in a neutral, matter-of-fact manner, as if none of it really affected her. Stu had never seen anyone so utterly defeated by life.

"Mrs. Blaisdell, did your husband keep any records that I could look at? It's very important to me to find out how much he was paid for that ghosting assignment."

"The records are gone."

"Gone?"

"Oh, yes. They vanished the day he was killed. Didn't you know that? He kept it all in a big ledger, and that was gone. It made it tremendously difficult to figure out things after he died. What money was due and so forth. But Mr. Gustavson was a great help in working it all out. One thing that helped was a habit Randy had that I always thought rather strange."

"What habit was that?"

"When he completed a manuscript, he would write the price he was paid across the front of the title page. And he usually kept his manuscripts, at least those that would appear in print under his own name."

"And did he keep copies of manuscripts he'd ghostwritten for others?"

"No, no, those he always disposed of. I can show you a few of his manuscripts, but they are all of books that appeared under his name."

"Had you talked to Marvin Fodor at all in the days before he died?"

"The very day before, but he didn't tell me anything that would help you."

"How did he seem?"

"Very excited. On top of the world, in fact, as though he'd made some discovery that would change everything around. I had the feeling he wanted to give me some good news but was restraining himself, for fear of building me up for a letdown. Not much chance of that actually."

The discovery of that copy of *The Atlantis Courier* in Vermilion's, Stu reflected. And after that he'd called Mrs. Blaisdell and Craig Kitchener. Who else would he have called? And who could have met him in the shop and killed him?

"I appreciate your talking to me, Mrs. Blaisdell," Stu said gently. "Is there anything else?"

"I don't know what would help you. But do you know what hurt Randy about the ghosting job for Arlen Kitchener even more than the money?"

"What?"

"Kitchener didn't even want to meet him. As if he didn't want to dirty his hands."

"You mean they never met?"

"No. All the negotiating was done through Clarence Gustavson."

"Kitchener appreciated your husband's work enough to recommend him to others."

"He may be a fine man. But he refused to meet Randy."

Daniel Vermilion seemed to look like the middle-aged teen-agers he had met in school: the smooth, round face, its sharp-pointed nose looking like a carrot in a snowman's head; the spoiled baby pout, the air of immature self-importance. It was a persona that seemed impossible to maintain into actual middle age. His wife, poor woman, seemed to be an obsequious drudge, hanging on his every word and every want. Something like Kitchener's wife, but without even a shred of dignity or individual identity. And Vermilion rudely waved her away as they sat down to talk.

"Would you like a glass of wine, Officer? It's a very nice vintage. Wine is a good investment mostly, but on occasion I like to drink some."

"Is my visit an occasion, Mr. Vermilion?"

"When I want a drink of this beautiful stuff, anything is an occasion. But that's okay, you're on duty, never mind, but how about some iced tea?"

"No."

"Then what can I do for you?"

"I'm working on the murder of a man named Marvin Fodor. It occurred in your late father's store. I assume you've heard about it."

"I don't often watch the news."

"Then you haven't heard about it?"

"It doesn't interest me very much. I never understood him. Great business sense, but no killer instinct. I suppose that's a poor choice of words. Someone had a killer instinct, eh?" He laughed hollowly.

Gonzales decided he really didn't like this guy.

"That store is a valuable piece of property. We weren't close, but I am his son. I could have sold it off quite nicely. The stock might even have been worth a bit, I'm told. I've never been into rare books myself. They're bulky and get dusty and their market value is damnably unpredictable. Stamps and currency are a little better. Art, now, is bulkier and more erratic still. I got heavily into gold at just the wrong time, you know that? My mother was a saint. She really knew how to negotiate a contract. Did you know she was in silent pictures?"

"I think I read something . . ." This guy was going to give him a headache.

"A beautiful woman. She died in a car wreck when I was two. I've collected prints of her films, though God knows *they* aren't valuable. I don't say she could act, but she was a beautiful woman and a great head for business."

"I'm looking for a manuscript, Mr. Vermilion."

"Manuscripts? They interest me even less than books."

"This particular manuscript was an autobiography that your father was working on when he died. About the book business and the authors he'd known."

"It damned well better be about the book business! There better not be anything about my mother in there."

"You haven't seen it?"

"No, but if it turns up, it belongs to me. Not to my bitch cousin Rachel. She inherited the store and the books, not any literary properties. I remember the way she used to kiss up to him whenever she came here to visit, really did a job on the old man. Not that I begrudge her anything. I met her at the airport when she came, offered her a place to stay, did all I could to make her feel welcome. But the money from unloading the store would have come in damned handy, especially after taking a bath on the gold." He waved a hand at his opulent Santa Monica living room. "I don't claim we're destitute here by any means. But I was his son, after all."

"Mr. Vermilion, I have to find out what happened to that manuscript. Edgar Ferris, your father's lawyer, went through it at the time of your father's death. According to him, it was turned over to you with other papers of your father's."

Daniel Vermilion raised a pudgy forefinger. "Got it! I sold the papers."

"You sold your father's papers?"

"Why not? Why the hell not, I ask you? What good were they to me? There was nothing there I could use." He gulped the white wine and poured another glass. "I sold them to that high school teacher."

"What high school teacher? What was his name?"

"Aw, I don't remember."

"When did you sell them?"

"I don't remember the exact date. I think it was before snotty Rachel came from Arizona—or maybe shortly after, I don't know. I remember thinking she probably would have wanted a look at them, bookish bitch that she is, but then they were mine and I had a price and I could sell them. I don't remember there was an autobiography in there, but there may have been."

"Was the teacher's name Marvin Fodor?"

"Oh, you mean the guy that got murdered? That might have been it. Suppose I describe him to you. Medium height, about forty, black hair, stocky build, close-trimmed beard."

"That sounds like Fodor. Was there a bill of sale?"

"Just a straight cash transaction. As far as I was concerned, he was hauling away junk."

"Did he say what he wanted the papers for?"

"Literary study for his students."

"High school students? What could they get out of studying the papers of a deceased book dealer?"

"Well, he had a lot of important customers."

"A few minutes ago, you seemed to have a pretty healthy idea of the literary value of your father's reminiscences. And yet you let this high school teacher haul this stuff away like so much junk? That doesn't fit in with your business sense, Mr. Vermilion, if you don't mind my saying so."

The aged teenager looked uneasy. "Well, it may have been an off day. Like the day I bought all that gold," he added with a tentative smile that Gonzales did not return.

"Suppose Fodor thought Vermilion's papers had something to do with the death of Ransom Blaisdell. This would be after Blaisdell's death, wouldn't it?"

"Who's Blaisdell?"

"Mr. Vermilion, I wish you'd cooperate with me. I think Fodor came to you, wanting a look at your father's papers to help him in his efforts to prove that Ransom Blaisdell ghostwrote a book for Arlen Kitchener."

"This is all Greek to me, Detective Gonzales."

"Come on, Vermilion, you might as well tell me the truth. I don't think we have anything on you anyway. I don't suppose

146

you've done anything illegal. Unless you killed Fodor yourself, and that doesn't seem likely."

"Me kill Fodor? What in hell are you talking about?"

"I said it was unlikely. But I think Fodor knew that Blaisdell habituated Vermilion's bookstore, and when Blaisdell died shortly after Vermilion he sensed a connection. He came and made a deal with you for Vermilion's papers, on the understanding that if anything came of it—like if he was successful in blackmailing Kitchener or whatever it was he was planning—you'd be in for a cut. The manuscript didn't say anything specific about Blaisdell's ghosting the novel. It led Fodor to go to Vermilion's to try to find some other evidence of the claim that Blaisdell wrote *The Atlantis Courier*. First he broke into and searched the store while it was closed. Still not convinced, he came back to check out Vermilion's after your cousin reopened it. He may have been told by Blaisdell that his rough manuscript of the novel, proving his authorship, was hidden somewhere in the store. Naturally, once Fodor was killed in the store, you were scared to come forth and tell us you'd made a deal with him for your father's papers. Now isn't that right?"

Vermilion swallowed. "Well, I can't speak to all of that, of course. But I did agree with this high school teacher I sold them to—and I suppose it might have been Fodor—that if any profit accrued from my father's papers, I would be entitled to a share. As you say, I haven't done anything illegal or dishonest, have I?"

"No, I don't think so. I'm going to bring you a picture of Fodor and see if you can identify him as the man you sold the papers to. Whether you wanted to or not, Mr. Vermilion, you've been very helpful. You've provided a link in the chain. Is there anything else you can tell me that might be helpful?"

"I'll try very hard to think about it, Detective Gonzales. Because I do want to help. I really do."

"Why couldn't you show me these yesterday?" Gonzales asked, looking at the two copies of *The Atlantis Courier* Rachel had put before him. "All you had to do was open them up and see."

"She's doing her best to help you," said the stocky guy next to her. She'd introduced him as Rod Wellman, apparently that reporter's brother. He fleetingly wondered if Rachel knew any women.

Rachel gave Rod a warning look. "I was very tired last night."

"All you'd have had to do was hand me the evidence. As it is, you've hung onto it overnight for no good reason." He tried to keep the irritation out of his voice, at least that part of it that represented the admiring male rather than the dedicated cop.

He added placatingly, "This is valuable, though. At this point, nobody is denying the authorship of *The Atlantis Courier*, but these can be helpful. And this figure $7,750 is certainly interesting, considering what that science fiction dealer told you. But if this is the price he was paid for the ghosting job, why would he write it in the book?"

"I don't really know," Rachel admitted. "But if this isn't the ghosting price, it would certainly be a big coincidence."

"Why did he sign so many copies?" Rod chimed in. "It just doesn't make sense. I can see him doing it once. But to actually cross out Kitchener's signature and replace it with his own. I just don't see it. If he was so angry, I'm surprised he didn't take it out on Kitchener directly."

"Maybe he couldn't," Rachel said uneasily. This conversation was starting to verge on dangerous ground. "He must have been really frustrated."

"Maybe he threatened Kitchener with blackmail," Rod mused. "But if he did that, he wouldn't want to leave around a lot of evidence that could give away the secret and blow his blackmail opportunity. And if he wanted to continue his activities as a ghost, he certainly wouldn't want to get the reputation as someone who would betray his customers. Either way you look at it, it just doesn't figure he'd go around signing his name to a bunch of copies of *The Atlantis Courier.*"

Calling on whatever reserves of telepathic power she might have at her disposal, Rachel filled the air with one message: *Rod, won't you please shut up?* But she didn't seem to be getting through.

The humoring expression on Gonzales' face, more than any messages he was getting from Rachel, brought Rod's speculations to a halt. "I guess everybody wants to be a detective," he said sheepishly.

"I appreciate your input, Dr. Wellman," Gonzales said politely. "Of course, one thing we'll do is to make sure these signatures are genuine, though I can't see any motive for their being forged. Thanks for your cooperation, Miss Hennings. Oh, there's one other thing. We've taken the guard off your store. Lieutenant's orders."

"The one who sits on his duff?" Rachel smiled.

Gonzales grimaced. "I don't like to comment on what my superior sits on. He says he just can't justify the manpower, and I suppose there's no real reason to think you're in any danger. Even if there's a copy of Blaisdell's version of *The Atlantis Courier* hidden somewhere in the store, that wouldn't seem too important now to anybody. But if you'd feel safer, you might want to close up the shop today."

"I don't think so," said Rachel.

Gonzales shrugged. "Whatever you think. I'll be checking with you whenever I can."

As the policeman left, Rachel dropped into a chair. The pulling of the guard didn't really frighten her, but she was alarmed at the idea Manny Gonzales might be suspicious of her. She had nothing to gain by faking the signatures, but after that song-and-dance about why she hadn't given him the two books last night . . .

Rod's voice brought her back to the present. "So how about it? I like to play detective as well as anybody, but why don't we just leave the sleuthing to Detective Gonzales and my crazy brother and go back to Tempe where we belong? I can't take a deep breath in this place."

Rachel didn't answer.

"If you're worried about the air controllers' strike, I hear that flying is just as safe now as ever. Maybe safer. There are some delays, of course, but . . ."

"Rod," she said, "why do you want to insult my intelligence and my dignity and my whole character by implying that if I wanted to marry you the air traffic controllers' strike would stop me? Why don't you just slow down and listen to what you're saying?"

Rod's face collapsed.

"Don't looked so damned pitiful. Sure you'd like to be felt sorry for, but a psychologist ought to know that's no basis for a

149

relationship anyway. We've established that you believe enough in going after what you want to make this wholly Don Quixote-ish trip from Arizona to here to try to get me to marry you. But that you have the idea that my similar strong feelings would be capable of upset by a strike of . . . I mean, we could take a bus, couldn't we? Or even a train. Doesn't Amtrak still run there? You seem to have a damn low opinion of me. And neither Stu nor I have felt we could tell you the whole story of what's going on here because you couldn't handle it. And I know that's true. And if I can't share things like that with you with confidence, what basis would that be for a relationship?"

"Things like what?" Rod looked totally baffled.

"If we'd told you, you wouldn't have screwed things up so completely with Detective Gonzales a minute ago. But if we'd told you, you'd have been out of here on your way back to Arizona, thinking we were both nuts!"

"Rachel, you're getting hysterical."

"And don't tell me I'm getting hysterical! Because I am in complete control of myself, and if I am raising my voice at this moment, it's because I choose to raise my voice. Some situations call for the raising of the voice, and this is one of them."

"Wait a minute, Rachel—"

"For what? Wait for what?"

"I think you're getting all excited far out of proportion to what I've done. Whatever it is that you think I've done, and I don't think I've done anything. You seem willing to confide in my brother, but ever since you've known him you seem to have had nothing but trouble. Maybe I never should have called him."

"If you called him to spy on me or act as some kind of guardian angel to me, then you're right. You shouldn't have. If you think your brother Stu has somehow not been true blue to the brotherly code, you can forget it, because he's been such a symbol of fraternal loyalty ever since I've known him, it's disgusting. What-ever could have happened between us has been hampered by it. I think both of you guys are living in the past, I really do."

"You said 'us' just then. Which 'us' do you mean?"

"Huh?"

"You and me us or you and Stu us? When you said us?"

"Rod, you're so predictable. There's more going on here than who takes who to the sock hop."

"What sock hop?" said Rod helplessly.

Rachel took a deep breath, shook her head a few times, and willed herself to calm down. "I'm sorry. I'm sure I'm being very unfair. But you're a psychologist, Rod. You know what happens to people who confront something they don't understand. Like ESP or UFOs."

"I wouldn't put ESP in that category. It's not my field of interest, but nowadays, not believing in ESP is like not believing in electricity."

"It's been mainstreamed, in other words," said Rachel, with an edge to her voice. "But what about UFOs?"

"Well, I guess people who see flying saucers or UFOs have seen something—at least, some of them have—but there's certainly no evidence that they come from outer space or anything like that."

"How do you feel about the study of them? The scientific study?"

"Well, it could be a waste of time. There could be nothing there to study."

"But ESP has enough scholarly verification to be respectable, right?"

"You know how academia is. If you try something too new, you're running a big risk as regards promotion and tenure. You want to do work that's original but not *too* original."

"And that doesn't bother you at all?"

Rod shrugged. "No, I don't see why it should. ESP is a little far-out for me, but I can respect colleagues who study it seriously. But stuff like UFOs—"

"Well, Rod, what is going on here is something really new, really unprecedented. I'd love to have the confidence of somebody ready to deal with it, explore it with me. And I'm not sure even Stu is ready to do that. And I think you are even less likely. Which is not to say there's anything wrong with you, Rod. Don't take it like that. I guess it's me that has the problem, and it's not the kind I can share with anybody. Not really."

Rod rose to his feet. "Rachel, I think I'll get back to Stu's. I

151

hope you'll think about what I said." He leaned over to give her a quick, sad kiss on the cheek and was gone down the stairs to the shop and out the back door.

Rachel watched him go.

16.

Craig Kitchener sat in his room contemplating the daily line on the old typewriter. He was starting to wonder just what it was he'd been doing the past few months with his compulsive raking of the coals. His father deserved whatever happened to him, of course, but his mother didn't, and any misery of his father would ultimately be shared equally. They were that much of a partnership.

Annie had given him a meaningful look that morning, but even screwing the maid under his father's roof had lost most of its savor. The old man hadn't talked to him since the night he'd made that damned phone call. He might never talk to him again, which wouldn't be so bad. But bringing that kind of misery on his mother—that he couldn't forgive himself for.

Every line he typed today looked like an old Al Jolson song lyric. Which at least fulfilled his subconscious qualification of writing nothing that had a market.

He heard a tapping on the door of his room. Probably Annie.

"Yeah?"

"It's your father," said a voice. "May I come in?"

"Yeah, come in," said Craig sullenly.

Arlen Kitchener looked better than he had any right to. In fact, he looked as though a load had been lifted from his shoulders. "I've just been talking to your mother. She knows everything now."

"It saves her reading it in the paper."

"I'm sure I deserve that, Craig. And I'm sure you feel your own behavior recently has been exemplary."

"No, I don't," Craig admitted.

"Your mother is still behind me, Craig. She's a wonderful woman."

"I can't argue with that."

"At least we have some common ground then. What I am going to say I am saying at her suggestion. I may have been too proud to come up with it myself, but I agree that it is something that needs to be said. And I am not going to apologize for what I write.

153

I believe in it, not as great literature but as more than adequate entertainment, something that adds something to other people's lives, that for a few moments lightens their burden."

"Refrain for violin and mixed metaphors," his son said.

"It is a measure of how confident I feel at the moment, Craig, that I am not angered by your sarcasm—"

"And are not now kicking my ass all over the room."

"That is correct. Nevertheless, I should have done a better job of getting to know you as you were growing up, of understanding and responding to your needs. Once I knew that the book of mine you admired was one I had not written, well, I should have done something. I'm not sure what. Perhaps I should never have considered using a ghostwriter in the first place. That was just an extension of my pride. And I want you to know that your activities, including the anonymous telephone call you made to provoke or frighten me, are in some measure understandable. Not admirable, certainly, but understandable. That they came to pass may well be as much on my heads as on yours."

"Who told you I made that call?"

"No one. But once I had this secret out in the open, I could begin to think clearly. And I knew that you were the most likely to feel strongly enough about the authorship of *The Atlantis Courier* to do that. I hope someday there may be a book actually written by me that will please you as much as that one did. But if that is a forlorn hope, so be it. For us to be father and son, you don't have to like my novels and I don't have to like your wretched poetry. Agreed?"

"It better be agreed, because it's not likely to change."

"Anyway, the bottom line, as the accountants say, is that your mother and I still love you, we don't hold anything you have done against you. And I apologize for anything that I have done to make your life more difficult or more complicated than it would otherwise have been."

In an almost inaudible voice, Craig said, "I'm sorry, too. I really am." He turned his face away.

"It was wonderful to find, as I ought to have known, that I could tell everything to your mother, and it wouldn't make any

154

difference. It was foolish of me, once I decided to employ a ghostwriter, to try to hide the fact from my family. That I did so has caused me much unnecessary anguish. I have prepared a statement for media, fully admitting the deception regarding *The Atlantis Courier*. It must be true that confession is good for the soul, for I feel wonderful. I also placed a call to Clarence Gustavson, firing him as my agent. He seemed to receive the news with equanimity. I bear him no animosity now, but I doubt that we could work together successfully in the future. I will try to find another agent with whom I am passably well matched. I talk a lot about my perfect matches, Craig, but really your mother is the only one. I have a title for my next novel, Craig. I'm going to call it *The Survivor*. I like the sound of that."

Craig Kitchener heaved his shoulders. A moment ago, he'd actually been moved by what his father was saying. They'd actually made contact. But now he seemed to have returned to completely commercial considerations. They'd never truly understand each other.

"I might even do a nonfiction piece on these murders, from the viewpoint of someone intimately involved. A nonfiction novel, as Capote calls them. Maybe you and I could collaborate on it, make it a sort of dual confession. What do you think? The Wallaces do that kind of thing all the time, with far less emotionally charged material than we could bring to the project."

"I'll think about that," Craig said. The old guy couldn't be serious. He felt his contempt welling up again. He couldn't help it. "But for now I'd like to get back to my work." He gestured at the manual typewriter.

"Certainly, Craig. You keep at it, and the rewards will come one day."

Craig was vaguely wondering what was for dinner.

"Oh, there was one other thing your mother and I discussed, Craig. And we reached a decision. We've decided to kick you out of the house. That was your mother's term. We think it would be good for you to be off on your own."

"You what?"

"Oh, don't worry. There's no hurry. You can take as much as a week to find another place if you want. And you have a standing dinner invitation for every Sunday afternoon. Let us know if there is anything we can do to help you move."

His father left the room with a devastating jauntiness to his step.

17. Rachel sat at the table in the back of the shop signing the name of Aldous Huxley to a very nice copy of *After Many a Summer Dies the Swan*. It was risky with the shop open for business and the possibility a customer might catch her in the act. Like the serial murderer who wants to be stopped before he can murder more, perhaps she wanted to be caught at it. She used those terms to herself and found it troubling, for she knew that no one could sign that name in that particular way except for Aldous Huxley himself, wherever he was.

Late afternoon had come and gone. It was starting to get dark outside, and she had not heard for hours from Stu or Rod or Manny Gonzales. She was sure Rod wasn't doing anything interesting, but she had no idea what the other two might be up to. Now she heard the door jingle at the front of the shop. A customer had entered, a heavy-set older man.

"Miss Vermilion?" he said.

"No, my name isn't Vermilion. I'm Rachel Hennings. Oscar Vermilion was my uncle."

"Of course. This shop has been the source of some rather interesting books lately, Miss Hennings."

"Yes, we have a lot of interesting books in stock," she said.

"Worrisome books," the man said. "Worrisome to me."

Rachel began to feel a twinge of alarm. "What do you mean?"

"It has to do with a simple business deal I entered into a few years ago. At least, it seemed simple at the time. But now, I don't know. I feel as though someone is trying little by little to destroy me on the basis of that business deal. I may be feeling a little paranoid, but there we are."

"Who are you?" she said.

"I'll explain in a moment," he said. "Do I hear a phone ringing?"

She listened. "Yes, in my apartment upstairs."

"Why don't we go answer it?"

"We?"

157

"Yes." He drew a small pistol from his pocket. "We. I suggest you close up the shop."

Rachel looked frantically out the front door. No one in sight. It was getting dark fast. She slowly put the CLOSED sign in the window, lowered the shade, and locked the door under the intruder's carefully watching eye.

The phone kept ringing. By the time she had reached the top of the stairs, the gunman prodding her all the way, it was on the tenth ring.

"You have a persistent caller."

"Do you want me to answer it?"

"On further consideration, no. Why don't we sit down?"

"Why don't you tell me who you are and what it is you want?"

"No, no, you misunderstand, Miss Hennings. Perhaps your reading has been too genteel. It's the man with the gun who asks the questions, not the gunnee."

"What do you want to know then?"

"I want to see whatever evidence you have about the financial dealings on *The Atlantis Courier*. Books, correspondence, a certain manuscript perhaps, anything relating to the deal between Kitchener and Blaisdell on that book."

"You're Clarence Gustavson?"

"Correct."

"And if I find you whatever other evidence exists, what will you do then?"

"Thank you kindly and leave. I don't intend to harm you."

"That's a nice thought, but I don't believe it for a second. Why are you coming after it with a gun in your hand? Why don't you just ask?"

"I don't need to account for my motives to you, Miss Hennings. You and Fodor must have had a smart little blackmail plan going."

"I didn't even know Fodor."

"Then why did he call me here to your shop to show me that book supposedly signed by Randy Blaisdell? Randy would never have done that, signed Arlen's book. It had to be a forgery. Who was the forger? You or Fodor?"

"I have a certain talent . . ."

"It's a talent all right. You could have fooled me with that signature if I hadn't known. And then that policeman Gonzales showed me another one today with a figure over it, and I knew this was all part of an elaborate ongoing shakedown. I don't have any idea how you came to know what you know, but I won't stand for it."

Rachel didn't know what to say. Obviously, the agent had killed Fodor and probably Blaisdell, too. To hide whatever he needed to hide—and it seemed clear it was more than just the authorship of *The Atlantis Courier*—he would have to kill her as well. He would have little choice. She wondered if he would be interested in an alternative.

"This talent of mine is pretty good. I can do all sorts of signatures. Maybe we could go into business together."

Gustavson laughed. "You seem to think I have a larcenous nature, Miss Hennings. I don't really. All I want to be is a good and successful literary agent. In a moment of weakness, I may have tried one criminal act, but I hardly expect to become a professional criminal."

"Isn't murder a criminal act?"

"I've maintained my amateur standing in that department, I'm sure. I did do a good job with Randy Blaisdell, though. I didn't really go there expecting to kill him, or that's what I like to tell myself. But since I went there in a rental car that I parked several blocks away, and entered the house through the back alley unseen by neighbors, as well as subtly disguising my appearance by not wearing my hairpiece, I suppose the possibility I might have to do something desperate must have crossed my mind. Arlen had told me there was something in your uncle's papers about the true authorship of *The Atlantis Courier*, and I questioned Blaisdell about whether he had revealed it. I know Arlen would be coming to see him, and the one thing that I could not have under any circumstances was a meeting between my two clients. Then they would have found out. . . . But you know all this, don't you?"

"You cheated on the ghosting fee. You charged one fee to

Kitchener and paid a smaller one to Blaisdell, pocketing the diffference. And the $7,750 written on the book must have been the fee you paid Blaisdell."

"My, my, you act as if you just figured that out. Very innocent."

"You murdered Blaisdell to keep him from revealing it. But it was just a few thousand dollars. And you and Kitchener were such good friends. Wouldn't he have understood? Was it so important that you'd commit murder to cover it up?"

"Arlen is not understanding about things like that. He has an obsession with business ethics. If he thought I'd cheated him of five dollars, let alone several thousand, it would have been the end of my brilliant career. He would have stopped at nothing to ruin me. You may find that hard to believe, but I've known Arlen Kitchener for a long time."

"But now both figures will be a matter of record. You're bound to be found out."

"The $7,750 appears nowhere except on the flyleaf of that book, where it can hardly be considered persuasive evidence. I took Randy's ledger and saw to it that figure could be found nowhere. Not even his widow knows I didn't pay him the $18,000 Arlen agreed to. But you and Fodor knew somehow. I think you must have seen a copy of Randy's manuscript. I think he must have written the figure he was paid for it on the title page, as was his eccentric custom, and then given the manuscript to Oscar Vermilion to keep for him. I think that was the reason Fodor foolishly had me meet him here, a second arrow in his quiver to go with the signed book, and I probably should have found that manuscript before I impulsively finished him off. I want to see it now. Where is it?"

Improvising desperately, Rachel said, "I was not involved in that end of things. I knew nothing about your financial pecadillos or about this supposed manuscript. My only job was forging the signatures. Marv took care of the rest of it. Look, Mr. Gustavson, you'll never get away with killing me. They're bound to be on to you by now. They have all the evidence, or will know where to look for it. But I could hide you here, and we could, oh I don't know, fly somewhere in disguise. I could forge signatures, and you could sell the books. I can do almost any signature. Would you like to see me? It's a marvelous talent."

"I would, actually." Gustavson smiled sardonically. "It's against my better judgment, of course, but my judgment hasn't been too good lately."

"You'll have to come back downstairs."

"By all means, let's, and perhaps you can also show me that manuscript, eh? The one you profess to know nothing about. But please don't make any unwise moves, Miss Hennings. It might make me and my friend here nervous."

"Stu, I tried to call Rachel a few minutes ago, and she didn't answer," Rod said as his brother came in the door of the apartment.

"She has a life of her own, Rod. Probably gone out with that Chicano cop again, huh?"

"Gonzales?"

"No, O'Malley. You better watch it, Roddy, he's liable to steal your girl. Anyway, the police guard is still on the shop, isn't it?"

"No. Gonzales told us they took it off earlier today. He was sure she wasn't in any danger. She isn't, is she, Stu?"

Stu looked worried. "Maybe we better get over there, huh? Just to make sure."

While speeding to Vermilion's, Stu confided his suspicions. "I'll be darned if I think I can prove it, but I think the agent, Gustavson, killed Fodor. Probably Blaisdell, too. And I think there may be a manuscript of *The Atlantis Courier* hidden somewhere in the store. Or, if there isn't, Gustavson will think there is, or some other piece of evidence that would reveal his swindle of Blaisdell and Kitchener. I wasn't worried about Rachel as long as I thought there was a guard on the store, but if there isn't . . . I just want to be sure Gustavson doesn't try something desperate."

When they pulled up in front of the shop on Santa Monica Boulevard, the light was still on in the window, but the CLOSED sign was in the door. It looked odd to Stu.

"I think I see somebody moving around in the back of the store," he told Rod in a whisper. "I didn't think Gustavson would be foolish enough to come here, but he may have panicked." Stu heard something in his own voice that sounded disquietingly like panic.

"Should we go around the back and try to get in there?" Rod suggested.

"I don't know what to say. We could just knock, but I don't know."

Rachel managed to sign a Faulkner and a Fitzgerald for Gustavson, and he was suitably impressed. But he was still standing there with the gun, and she wasn't sure what she should do next to amuse him. She could suggest they both search for the manuscript, but she doubted Gustavson would buy that. If only she could warn someone. Finally she decided that if she could switch the lights off suddenly and dive under the heavy wooden table, she could protect herself from his fire and maybe cause enough of a ruckus to attract somebody's attention. Where were all her ardent suitors when she needed them anyway?

Probably he wasn't that great a shot with a handgun. Still, he'd presumably used that same weapon on Marvin Fodor.

Manny Gonzales was worried.

Gustavson's secretary had admitted her boss was acting strangely that day. The records said the ghosting price on *The Atlantis Courier* had been $18,000. Manny couldn't prove the $7,750 was the actual price paid, and the testimony of Rachel's friend Blast-Off Meegher was hardly what he'd call court-worthy, but the figure had to mean something. Blaisdell had to have some reason to write it there.

He felt he had to locate Gustavson, talk to him again. But he couldn't find him. He drove toward Vermilion's with a feeling of unreasonable panic rising in him. Maybe the agent would go after Rachel. Maybe he'd had some hint about the Blaisdell manuscript and thought it was still hidden in the store. They never should have taken that guard off

As Stu was reaching the back door, he saw the lights in Vermilion's go off suddenly, then heard a thump and a gunshot, closely followed by a scream. He rattled the back door helplessly, totally innocent of any weapon to help him open it or get to Rachel.

At the front door, Rod managed to kick in the glass and blunder into the store. But he couldn't distinguish friend from foe in the darkened shop. He fell over the 50¢ book rack and wound up on his back. He thought he felt a bullet whiz by the top of his head, but it appeared to do no damage. Suddenly the store was flooded with light.

A big man he didn't know was standing there looking around like an enraged bull. He'd found the light switch, but where was Rachel?

Gustavson fired again in Rod's direction and Rod skittered across the floor. He saw his brother coming up behind Gustavson from the rear, but Gustavson whirled and clouted Stu on the jaw with his pistol. Then he lurched toward the front of the shop, looking wild-eyed for Rachel.

Rod was wondering what to do next when he felt or heard a rumbling in the shop. A California earthquake, was his first thought. Some of the shelves were teetering. He covered his head with his hands and waited for the end—a collapsed ceiling or a bullet from the big guy's gun.

That was when a whole range of shelves separated itself from the wall and collapsed on Gustavson, pinning him to the floor. The agent roared with a combination of shock, frustration, and pain. He involuntarily loosened his grip on the handgun, which went skittering across the floor toward Rod. When he could summon the presence of mind, Rod leaped to his feet and grabbed the pistol. A snowfall of sheets of yellow paper seemed to be filling the store, apparently freed from their resting place behind some of the books on a high shelf. Rod stumbled toward the rear of the shop, dodging the debris. Rachel had appeared from somewhere and was already bending over Stu's inert form.

As Gonzales pulled his unmarked car up to the front of Vermilion's, he nearly collided with a patrol car. Two uniformed officers came out with guns drawn.

"What's going on?" he said. "I didn't call you guys."

One of the patrolmen recognized him. "We got a call somebody heard shots in there. Sounds quiet now."

"The front door glass is broken," Gonzales pointed out. "Come on. Let's get in there."

Before they could, the door swung open and a disheveled trio appeared. Stu Wellman, seeing the guns in the patrolmen's hands, raised his arms in mock surrender.

"Enough firearms," he groaned.

"What the hell happened in there?" Gonzales demanded.

"It's Gustavson," said Rachel. "You'd better call an ambulance."

One of the patrolmen rushed to his radio.

"But what happened?" Gonzales asked, going past them toward the door.

"It was an earthquake, wasn't it?" said Rod.

"If it was, we didn't feel it out here."

"But a whole shelf of books fell on him. Just came away from the wall and fell on him," said Rod. "How did that shelf come away from the wall if it wasn't an earthquake? Do you have so many earthquakes out here you locals don't even notice them?"

A few minutes later, after Gonzales had given the injured Gustavson what first aid he could and also assured himself that the agent was safely immobilized, he and Rachel and the Wellman brothers resumed their post mortem in front of the shop. Rachel handed him a sheet of the yellow paper that had dispersed itself all over the store.

It was a title page:

THE ATLANTIS COURIER

by

Ransom Blaisdell (for Arlen Kitchener)

140,000 words

And scrawled in pen was the familiar figure: $7,750!

"That's what Fodor was looking for," Rachel told them. "It was here after all, just as Blast-Off thought it might be. The night that Fodor met Gustavson here, he wanted to show him the signed copy, steal it, and maybe have Gustavson help him search for this manuscript. He'd tried to find it before, when the store was closed, but he hadn't really satisfied himself it wasn't here. I don't think he realized he was handing Gustavson a motive for his own murder. He didn't know anything about the way Blaisdell's agent had cheated him. Blaisdell didn't either. Poor Fodor just wanted the truth to be known about the book's authorship and to get some money for Blaisdell's widow. He'd contacted Kitchener's son for the same reason. I don't think he was a blackmailer, just a very blundering good samaritan who thought an opening up of the whole situation would lead to some help for Mrs. Blaisdell."

"How had your uncle hidden the manuscript?" Gonzales asked.

"I don't think there's any way to know. The pages started raining down when that shelf came away from the wall. The manuscript was probably on a tall shelf behind some books where they wouldn't be noticed even if someone took a book off the shelf to look at. Fodor would have found it eventually during his first trip to burglarize the store. But he wasn't a professional burglar and was probably very nervous, and anyway, how long would it take to remove all the books from the shelf to look behind them? I know he must have realized he hadn't looked in every possible place. If I were looking for it, I'd have tried for some inside joke of my uncle's, like hiding it behind the ghost stories of Algernon Blackwood."

"This place has nothing but ghost stories," Stu muttered.

"I think Blaisdell probably knew where Uncle Oscar had hidden it. There was no reason why he shouldn't. Uncle Oscar probably told him. Certainly Uncle Oscar wouldn't have wanted anyone else to know about it. If Blaisdell hadn't died, he'd have been in a position to retrieve the manuscript himself. He probably told Fodor that he'd given it to Uncle Oscar, but he had no reason to tell Fodor exactly where it was hidden in the shop."

She turned to look at Stu. "Are you okay? You got quite a bump on the head."

Stu reassured her, but the look that passed between them didn't reassure either Rod Wellman or Manny Gonzales. The professor and the cop looked at each other resignedly.

"I wonder if anybody runs a middle-of-the-night flight to Phoenix," Rod said, mostly to himself.

18.

The morning after, Vermilion's looked like a disaster area. Stu came downstairs first and tried to think of a way to save Rachel the appalling sight of books strewn all over the floor, bookcases toppled over and in some cases leaning on each other. He shook his head and reentered the apartment. Rachel was sitting up in bed and looking at him cheerfully.

"You have any idea what it looks like down there?" he asked. "Like a hurricane hit the place. You don't want to stay in the book business, do you?"

"Stu, how can you look so depressed? Gustavson's under lock and key, and the whole thing is over. Shelves can be put upright. Books can be reshelved. It's not the end of the world."

"I'm glad you feel that way," he said. "You seem resilient as all hell, but I'm suffering from an emotional hangover. Hangovers run in my family, but at least most of them are preceded by the pleasure of drinking."

"I think you're just unhappy because your knight-to-the-rescue bit didn't come off as you hoped. But I appreciated your intentions, and Rod's efforts didn't do any better." She smirked.

"I'm supposed to be happy because incompetent heroics run in the family?" Stu shook his head. "Look, let's slip out the back and I'll take you out to breakfast, and then maybe we can go away for a few days. A pal of mine has a cabin up in Idyllwild, and I can get some time off from the paper."

"What about the shop? I can't just leave all those books strewn everywhere. After what they did for me, it wouldn't be fair."

"What they did for you?"

"Falling on Gustavson like that."

"You're giving credit to your literary ghosts for that, huh? I hope none of them injured their writing wrists in the melee."

"Are you trying to pick a fight, Stu? I don't feel like fighting, but if you can think of any other explanation for that whole shelf falling on Gustavson just at the right moment, not to mention that Blaisdell manuscript putting in an appearance, I'd like to hear what it is. Forget Rod's earthquake theory. If there was an earthquake, neither the Richter scale nor the radio news knew anything about it. So, come on, what's your theory?"

"Termites."

She laughed. "No, seriously."

"With all that running around and violence going on in the store, who knows what might upset those old shelves? I don't think we have to blame a poltergeist committee from old Hollywood for it. And as I understood the chain of events, your uncle found out about Blaisdell just about the time you visited his shop for the last time as a teenager. You could have found out and subconsciously stored up the knowledge, only to have it release itself."

"Same old theory, huh? You won't let go. But that still makes me a forger, don't you see? A clever forger, but a forger. I don't want to be California's answer to Thomas J. Wise, Stu. I think we should really get those signatures tested. By a handwriting expert with every kind of scientific test possible, not just an inspection by sight."

"That figure above the last Blaisdell signature, too?"

"Well, I'm not sure I want that tested, but the signatures anyway. And if I'm forging them, it will become apparent, no matter how damn clever my subconscious is. How about that?"

Stu shook his head. "Naw, you might just as well sell them off. One of us would just have to admit he was wrong when the tests came through."

"Admit *he* was wrong?"

"He or she. And I think your having to admit you were wrong would damage our relationship."

"And what if you had to admit you were wrong?"

"That would destroy it completely. You know, I love you, but I guess I said that a few times last night." He made the admission almost reluctantly.

"I think you're still worried about Rod. He's on his way back to Tempe by now, and you're here, and you still have that old compunction about stealing your brother's girl. Stu, you belong in another time. You can't accept phenomena you don't understand. You have old-fashioned ideas about love and possession. You think a man on a white horse should rescue a damsel in distress, and you can't recognize victory when it hits you in the face. Now will you come downstairs and help me start sorting through the rubble? When we're finished, we can open up that bottle of champagne you brought me. The one we were saving for a festive occasion."

"And this is it? That festive occasion?"

"What's more festive than being in love? Now come on, let's get to work."

"Okay. But can't we just have a cup of coffee first?"

"Downstairs. In the easy chairs."

"Does that mean you have to pour Nathanael West a cup, too?

In the hours and hours of painstaking reshelving of the stock of Vermilion's bookstore, an odd fact emerged. Not one book was damaged, not one spine broken, not one page dog-eared. Even the works of Arlen Kitchener had come through the torrent unscathed.

If you have enjoyed this book, you might wish
to join the Walker Mystery Society.

For information, please send a postcard or letter to:

Paperback Mystery Editor

Walker & Company
720 Fifth Avenue
New York, NY 10019